Francis William Lauderdale Adams

Leicester

An Autobiography: Vol. II.

Francis William Lauderdale Adams

Leicester
An Autobiography: Vol. II.

ISBN/EAN: 9783337117535

Printed in Europe, USA, Canada, Australia, Japan

Cover: Foto ©Raphael Reischuk / pixelio.de

More available books at **www.hansebooks.com**

LEICESTER

.

An Autobiography

BY

FRANCIS WILLIAM L. ADAMS

' A rimirar lo passo
Che non lasciò già mai persona viva
DANTE

IN TWO VOLUMES
VOL. II

LONDON
GEORGE REDWAY
YORK STREET, COVENT GARDEN
1885

CONTENTS OF VOL. II.

LEICESTER.

~~~~~

III.—*continued.*

CHAPTER IV.

THE next day after lunch, I went for a walk to Hampstead, and wandered about there, my thoughts alternating between the beautiful soft nature about me and the past days of my first London weeks, till half-past six. Then I remembered that Rosy would be waiting for me at eight. It used to take me something under an hour to get from Maitland Street to Hampstead. It was now half-past six. What to do with myself for an hour?—from seven to eight, that was. Then my thoughts turned off in memory: memory of the many times I

had come marching along this very pavement in those first London days whose
second half was an age of weariness and
woe. Here was the very corner at which
I stood that dreary day. Was it all a
dream? 'I stand still here to-day,' I said
to myself, 'as I stood still here that day,
and look at the brown cracked concrete of
the low wall and the black sooty rails that
top it. The windows are lampless too, as
they were when I first stood still here.
Will the left one light up suddenly too as
it did then? No. Lampless yet. Who
lives here? God knows! And yet, foolish
though it be, will not the thought occur
again: '*Is it nothing to you, all ye who pass
by, my weariness and my woe?*' I put my
hand on the nearer cemented gate-post,
brown and cracked like the low wall, and
think of the figure that leant against it in
that dreary rain of half-darkness when my
body seemed all bloodless, and the girl
hurried by me with her huddled-up dress
and umbrella spread over her. I see her

now. Her quick glance, and that hurry
by : the devil that rose in me——

The door above opened and an old lady
came out and, looking at me through the
spectacles on her elevated nose, asked :

'Do you want anything, young man ?'

I took off my hat and held it off.

'Nothing,' I said gravely, ' thank you.
I hope my stopping a moment to examine
your gate-post has not troubled you,
madame ? I see that the cement is cracked
and peeling off. Now I am the patentee of
a cement which is warranted to——'

'No,' she said, looking at me over the
spectacles of her depressed nose, 'I don't
want any of your cement, thank you.
Good-day.'

And was in and viewing me suspiciously
through the glass door-panel of the closed
door. If I had not been afraid of disturb-
ing her feelings, I should have given a
shout. As it was, I repressed the shout,
and marched off quickly, laughing to myself.

22—2

It was a little past seven when I reached the canal bridge at the bottom of Maida Vale. I stayed a little there, looking at the flowers, finally buying a rose, and carrying it off with me. This I took to No. 3, and inquired of Mrs. Smith if Miss Howlet was in? She wasn't : as I expected. I left the rose, and went for a prowl about the streets.

All at once I found myself looking at the Marble Arch clock, by which it was five minutes past eight. Away I went up the Edgware Road, and was marching along at full speed, a little past Praed Street on the right side, when, passing before a gas-flaming fruiterer's, my eye took in a girl's form, and by the time I had gone five or six yards my heart was up in my throat at the sudden thought of—*Rosy !* I turned back at once. We met face to face, she smiling up into mine, I looking with an odd half-graveness into hers.

'Well,' she said, 'you *were* in a hurry !'

We were walking on together, I taking one stride to her two. It seemed to me odd in someway, this meeting. We had not shaken hands. I did not know what to say. We walked on together for a little in silence. Then I said:

'I am very sorry. You took me so by surprise. We have not shaken hands yet. And I hope you are well. Will you shake hands now?'

I stopped: and our right hands met, while my left held my hat off, and my eyes looked into hers. There was light upon it, not much light, from a parallel shop-window. The people passed on about us. There was no doubt that the child's face was very—pretty. We walked on again, I taking one stride to her two, as before. I said:

'I am very glad to see you. And I hope you are well. If you have taken walks, as you told me you would, then I am sure you are better than you were when I left you.' And began to think about the

words of Rayne's letter (where she stood
upright in the boat with head bared and
revelled in the light and the air and the all
of that new glory over everything) in connection with my bare head before this child's
face. The memory spoilt it. Rosy had
said something which I had not heard.

We talked of general things that did not
interest me or, I think, her much; till we
came to the corner of Maitland Street.
Then ensued questions and explanations,
and, in about five minutes, Rosy returned
from her visit to No. 3, full of the beautiful
rose I had given her.

'Beautiful rose?' I said. '. . . How
do you know *I* gave it you?'

'Because,' she answered,—'who else
would?'

She was ready for the walk now. We
set off at once, in a half-mechanical way
Park-wards, beginning to talk like two
children.

All at once:

'Here's your locket!' she said, taking it

from inside her coat, and holding it out, little and round and silver.

'Nay, yours :' I said. 'Not mine.'

'You gave it me, though.'

'I did. That made it yours.'

'But it *was* yours ; before that, or how could you have given it me ?'

I acquiesced, with the reflection that Adam must have had some trouble to get an authentic account of the eating of a certain historical apple.

'What are you laughing at ?' said Rosy.

'Have you forgotten the Swallow Song ?'

'Forgotten it ? My gracious, no !

'" She comes, she comes, the swallow,
    bringing beautiful hours,
    beautiful seasons.
    White on her——"

what *are* you laughing at ?'

It was no wonder she asked. Peal after peal of laughter, quenchless, re-echoing, came from me. The more I tried to stop it, the more it came. At last I stood still, exhausted, with my hands on my hips. But a glimpse of her face was enough to generate a fit of laughter as violent as the first. We went on together somehow or other, I still shaking with this second fit, she solemn to degree. All at once it struck me that she was a little afraid I was mad. I tried to assure her that there was nothing the matter with me but—laughter !

Well, I settled down at last : and then came the task of appeasing Rosy's outraged sense of dignity. I was, of course, really sorry to have laughed in this way. I explained that what had made me begin was the way she scampered over the Swallow Song . . . and so on.

Her outraged sense of dignity took a great deal of appeasing, but I managed it in the end. Nay, I pleaded so hard, that I obtained from her a repetition of the Swallow Song, repeated as we sat on that seat not far from the top, which I knew so well, so well, and perhaps she remembered.

We parted at the door of No. 3 at about eleven.

As I marched away down the Edgware Road, I thought of the evening I had spent with her, and of her grave bow of the head as I went back from her at the door with my hat down in my hand ; but, going across the Park, other thoughts came to me, and I had lost sight of the evening I had spent with her when I reached home.

Here the Journal begins again :

' Oh, Claire, Claire, that we should have met here in the time of eternity, and so parted ! Shall I ever forget the depth and sorrow of the eyes that were for that short hour as the air of my world ? Claire, Claire. Oh, it is a vile devil's earth, and good is only in the slave. To have held thee in my arms, and, with my eyes in thine, to have kissed thee once, and died. Death were sweet so.—But it is useless to think. This city is a market where souls are pledged for bodies, and bodies for souls, and wealth

buys all. I will go out from it. It is useless to think.

'There is a poor devil outside playing
furiously on a cornet, and an Italian girl
yaaing to her native concertina. A sweet
harmony! Not unlike my disgust. Jam
satis! Nay, jam nimium! I am a damnable idiot!'

It was a few days after this that Rosy
and I went our second evening walk together. There is no allusion to it in the
Journal, and as I was during most of it in
more or less of a half-dreamy, half-abstracted
state, I cannot remember much of what we
said. That walk was not what might be
called a success. We went up to the top
of Primrose Hill again, and I snuffed in the
breeze and was somewhat revived; but (it
had been raining heavily earlier in the day)
that made me appreciate how stickily muddy
it was going down, and I was forthwith
driven into a state of utter saplessness and
disgust. Rosy mocked at me as well as she

could, but I took no heed. Finally she declared she wouldn't walk with me any more. (This was half-way down the St. John's Wood Road.) I acquiesced. We stood still, I looking in front of me at nothing in particular, not thinking of offering my hand. Then she was turned and walking away. I did not look at her. When she had got some twenty yards, I looked at her with a comical smile : and sighed : and hit my iron-tipped stick-end straight on the way : and said a little wearily, ' Oh dear !' and went with large strides after her.

I caught her up in a little, and we walked on together in silence ; till I observed:

' I'm sorry I was rude—if I *was* rude.'

' Then you *were* rude then !' said Rosy.

' Rudeness implies deliberation,' I said. ' My definition of sin is : the deliberately doing anything that may harm anyone else. Thus, it is sin to buy a pistol, intending to kill, and then absolutely killing, a man : or, to ruin your body by excess, intending to beget, and then absolutely begetting, children.'

'You talk great stuff,' said Rosy.

'My dear child,' I answered, 'I intended you to apply my definition of sin to the point at issue, my rudeness or unrudeness. But this, like so many good intentions, has gone to the artificial protection of infernal causeways.'

Rosy vouchsafed no reply.

I proceeded :

'Well, be that as it may, considering the inability of the feminine intellect to comprehend anything of subtle in the matter of metaphysical psychology, or anything else you like, I shall proceed to admit that I *was* rude : and apologize accordingly.'

'*I* never asked you to apologize,' said Rosy.

'*I* never said that you did, my dear— well, something or other.'

'You're very aggravating to-night. That's what you are.'

'Oh, Polyphemus and Abracadabra, did you ever hear such a libel as that?'

Rosy began to hum a tune shortly and defiantly.

After a little I said gravely:

'Lady, it seemeth unto mine uncultured ear that thou warblest the melody of which men say the venerable vaccine one rendered up the ghost. Now——'

'You're very cruel!' suddenly sobbed Rosy. 'And I hate you. Why do you go on at me like that? . . .' (The rest inarticulate.)

'God bless my soul!' said I, standing still. 'If——' And I proceeded in a brotherly way to comfort her.

And so I at last got her in a rather limp state to No. 3, where we said a final good-night after I had promised to write and tell her when I could get time to go for another walk.

If it had not been for my recalling friend Horace to the effect that Dulce est desipere in loco, I should have, I think, been in a most disconsolate humour going home. As it was, I could not help laughing at the memory of our little squabble.

The next entry in the Journal is a record of my having seen, or thought I had seen, at a theatre the girl of the nuts, she who struck me so on the night of my interview with Colonel James. (She was playing a second part in a 'realistic drama,' and not playing it badly, it seemed to me.)

'I was with the Strachans in a box made for two people to see comfortably in, and three others to be as miserable as they disliked. I asked the Professor, when we two went out for a stroll in the passages during an entr'acte, if he had seen her before, and he said that he had not.

'I should like to know her. She might marry me perhaps, and then I should be properly miserable for the rest of my life, if I didn't murder her or she me before the honeymoon was over. Well, the original expression holds all right, even then. I wouldn't much mind her murdering me, I think, if I was only sure she'd be hanged afterwards. I have thoughts of proposing to Connie. She is a sweet little cocotte, only wanting development. But it would be better fun to marry Isabel, and see what could be done in the way of ruffling her " grave sweetness " a little.—I'll stop here.'

My feeling towards the book was, at the end, nothing short of positive loathing. Strachan I think perceived this ; for he did all he could to lighten my share of the work. And I accepted his doing so without remark. I remember his asking me one morning if I hadn't been a little out of my sorts of late, and my answering, with all solemnity, that my bowels were not as they used to be, and that I feared I had trichinosis. Pork, especially in the form of sausages, was a favourite dish of mine. (I never eat pork and particularly loathe sausages.) I don't know what he thought of my answer. He said nothing.

Late on in June is the next entry in the Journal :

' *Last night.*—

' Something making me come back quickly from the corner of the street, I found that she had not opened the door with her key yet : or even taken the key out of her pocket ; but was standing watching me seriously. I took off my hat, and stepped close to her with it in my hand. The moon was shining clear.

' Neither of us spoke. We looked into one another's eyes.

' At last :

' " What made you such a serious little rosebud to-night ?" I said.

' She sighed softly :

' " . . . I don't know."

' " Good-night, Rosy."

' " Good-night."

' " Good-night !" turning, I repeated to

myself, and put on my hat, and strode away.

' Round the corner, and I drew a breath of relief.—*That was temptation.*

' *I will not see that child again.*'

IV.

CHAPTER I.

It was four days after this, a Wednesday as I see, that I awoke at about half-past eight in the morning and found that there was a letter with my cup of tea. After a while I summoned up sufficient energy to pull the letter somehow from the table to onto the bed, and then must have fallen off into a doze again; for I remember that the writing of the envelope that must have been just under my half-closed eyes, was wound with some other writing in and out of a fantastic sort of dream-space from which I suddenly started, with the recognition that the letter was *Payne's*.

With all my soul in my eyes, I stared

at it. A large white glaring envelope
with

> ' B. LEICESTER, ESQ.,
>> *Colchester School,*
>>> *Colchester.'*

in Rayne's hand, in the middle, the last
three words lined through, and below in a
thin scrawly hand :

> ' 5, *Dunraven Place,*
>> *Piccadilly,*
>>> *London.'*

These details realized, I calmly took the
envelope, ripped it up at the back, produced the thick white folded double sheet
inside, and opened it. This is something
like what I read :

> ' 22, Balmoral Street, W.

' MY DEAR BERTRAM,

> ' We are in London for a short
time—three or four weeks, before going
north to spend the summer at Kirkory, my

husband's family seat, or I should say home. I have wondered a little at hearing nothing from you. You are, at the least, two letters in my debt. I do not even know where you are, and address this at random. I need not say, my dear Bertram, how pleased I should be to see you again; but I am afraid you have quite forgotten me. Why it is—how long is it, since you last wrote to me? I last heard from you at Montenotte in the autumn of —! How long ago is that? You ought to be ashamed to think!

'But here is time and space and patience (yours) all exhausted. I must end, as usual, in a hurry. Write to me and tell me what you are doing. You know that, if for no other reason than because you were loved by what I loved best in the world, you are and always must be dear to me: and so let me write myself down as being what, I trust, I always shall be,

'Your friend,

'RAYNE GWATKIN.'

I lay still for a time and thought about what I had read, and then re-read it, and thought of the past that concerned all this strange present, and of my whole life. And at last got up and went to my small polished-oak box (a small box in which I kept certain things that were, or had once seemed, precious to me), and, having opened it, found a letter, which began :

'MY DEAR BERTRAM,

     ' It is a wet and tempestuous afternoon, and therefore I consider it a fitting occasion to answer your long and with difficulty decipherable epistle.'

Through this letter I glanced, till I came to words that stopped my glancing and steadied it :

    '. . . Rather a tempest going on outside, and so I am going to try to dodge my dear old daddy and Sir James, and get out my boat and enjoy it.—By-the-bye, I had forgotten to tell you that an old friend of ours, Sir James Gwatkin, has been staying with us this last week. He is a most amusing mondain en villégiature, with a marvellous French and Italian accent, and altogether a very amusing companion to the father, and myself at times. He knows what seems to me a great deal about . . .'

And I folded up the letter and put it into the box, and re-locked the box, and went back to bed: and lay thinking for another half-hour, when I got up and dressed.

At breakfast I reconsidered the matter:

The news amounted to this: Rayne had married the amusing mondain en villégiature, and was here, in London, for a short time—three weeks or so, before going north to spend the summer at Kirkory, her husband's family seat or home. Where was Mr. Cholmeley?

I started:

'*Dead!*'

'That could not be. . . . And yet——'

I took out her letter and considered it.
' " You know that—if for no other reason
than because you *were loved* by what I *loved*
best——" Nay, that may be nothing : or
only mean that she *loves* her husband best.
And there is no black edge on this white
sheet. " By what I loved best in the world,
you are and always must be dear to me :
and so let me write myself down as being "'
(I hurried) ' " what I trust I always shall
be, your friend, Rayne Gwatkin."—It is
puzzling !'

All at once I exclaimed :

' She oughtn't to have married that
man !'

' . . . *Why?*' said the faint voice of the
air and the room. I answered to myself :
' *I wish she hadn't.*'

' . . . *Why?*' said the same faint voice.
I frowningly considered a few moments, and
then rose, a little viciously. Some of the
viciousness was expended in the sharp
putting of my chair directly in front of my
plate : the rest in my casting myself into

the arm-chair in the window, and, with my
hands at my mouth, scraping my lower lip
with my upper teeth. My eyes were half-
filled with tears as I looked out of the
window. My hand fell on to the chair-
arm, and some of the water in my eyes
welled out.

Then :

' What is the matter with me ?' I said to
myself ; and, after a pause : ' I don't know.
I wish I knew what was the matter with
me. Is there anything, then, in the whole
world would make me happy ? I don't
know. I don't think so. I'm just weary
of it all ! O wretchedness of disbelief in
everythirg ! What of that new soul's life
of mine, produced before Starkie, and believed in then! O my God ! what a miserable
devil I am ! What have I done ? What
shall I do ? What do I believe in ? What
do I doubt about ? *Everything : even
doubt.*'—I let my thoughts rest for a
moment.

Then :

'If I only *knew* something! If I only *loved* something! Oh, is there not a woman in the whole wide world who would take me as I am, and help me to be what I want to be? A *woman* to save *me*? Oh, God, God, God, God, I would I had never been born!—Nay, is it not strange that, in an hour of weakness like this, the only thing I cry out to for help is what I have always thought I despised as being itself incarnate weakness—*woman!* I don't know what's the matter with me. I'm not myself. Virtue is gone out of me. This must be a passing humour. I shall be strong again, as I used to be. *Or was it that I did not know my weakness?* . . . I don't know.' A complete sense of loneliness and purposelessness seemed suddenly to grow like a great grey-cut chasm in me. I could struggle no more to find out what was the matter with me. I turned and let the current take me where it would.

From that depth of weariness I raised myself a little to take up a book off the table beside me and read it. It was no good staying stretched on the bottom of that dark submarinity in that way. Better kill myself at once, and that most certainly I would not do. . . . Why not? I was afraid of death? I didn't know. I had not thought about it. I would not think about it. A piano-organ was playing outside. I opened the book, *A Tale of Two Cities*, and began to read at one of the last chapters.

The reading of it to the end stirred me considerably, enough to send the humour of weariness and purposelessness out of me. I felt this as, my under-thoughts full of Sydney Carton and envy of his death, I looked out into the sunshiny day; for some little of the sunshine had entered in me even then. I would go out for a walk. Nay, I would go and see where Rayne lived. Why not?

Away I went, and out for my walk— out and away to beautiful summer Hampstead, fresh and green from the late showers, in the soft early-day lights. I did not think much of Rayne. I do not remember what I thought of : probably of hundreds of unconnected things, passing in a fairy-procession in the yellow-gold light before my eyes. I wandered about happily till about one o'clock, when hunger made itself perceptible, and I went off in the pursuit of bread and fruit and milk. Followed another Pythagorean feast on the grass, with delightful half-dreams as in the old time ; till it occurred to me to return home and read. Accordingly, after a little trifling with resolution in the shape of dawdling about in hollows, looking at a small stream's meandering water, or the serried grasses and the earth, I fairly set off.

After a little, it occurred to me again to go and take a look at Rayne's house. So I asked the next bobby I saw where Balmoral Street was, and learnt that it was on this side of the Park, and, more particularly, close by Lancaster Gate, for which I had better ask. That was all I wanted at present. I set off again, and was in Maida Vale before I was aware of it. I had no idea of going to see Rayne to-day : I only wished to look at the house.

I went on seriously enough, and began to think about Rayne ; where she was now and what she was doing ? somehow as if I had wondered about some other woman some time and somewhere ; till my old faint far-away tremulousness came into me and was perceived.

I came sharply round an area railed corner, and beheld . . . a low carriage and horses, two footmen, the pillars of an exit into the street, a lady just out of the open door — on to the top step — descending. Rayne ; I stood still.

Some one followed. Rayne was on the pavement, making for the low carriage door, now held open. Stopped a moment : half turned. And the some one following was in her view and mine. It was the mondain en villégiature : I knew him. But Rayne's

face was all to me ; and yet I could not see
it properly. Then our eyes met.

Somehow or other I was moving to her
with my hat in my hand, and she said :
'Bertram !' and I had stood still again.

Her face was, perhaps, as it were worn.
I only knew that it was filled with the half
light of steadfastness, and that her eyes were
quiet and deep. I had seen, not her face,
but her face's form, and, as it were the half
light of it before, and this memory was on
me now almost as in the dim low distance
of a dream. I cannot say what either she
said, or he or I for a little; not that I was
bewildered by their presence and its thoughts
with me, but that this memory of the likeness
to the half-light of her face, perhaps kept me
in the dim low dream-distance.

At last I had shaken hands with the
mondain, and she was sitting in the carriage
and we two standing by the low back-opened
carriage door, talking together.

'It was, indeed, a surprise to see you in
London,' she was saying. 'I thought you

were . . . In fact I did not know what to
think, for you did not answer either of the
letters I sent to you——'

'Letters, Lady Gwatkin?' I said. 'I
received no letter from you, excepting this
morning, since November — two years
ago.'

'I am a witness to the writing of at
least two,' said he, looking at me with a
little smile round the corners of his mouth.

'Then you did not know—' she said . . .
'And I had wondered why you had not
written to me. . .'

'That Mr. Cholmeley was dead—' I
said softly, perceiving that her dress was
of black. 'I feared so this morning.'
What sorrow was in me for her was given
in the words here.

'And where have you been all this
while?' she said, looking up : 'if I may
ask?'

I bowed my head.

'I left Colchester last February. I was
in London for a little, and then in Paris

for a little, and then in London again till now.'

'Perhaps,' he said, 'Mr. Leicester would go with you a little way? You must have a great deal to say to one another after so long and so silent a separation?' I saw or thought I saw, that she did not desire that I should go with her. Half-hesitation of hers was not enough to entice me. I said :

'I am afraid that, even if Lady Gwatkin should be so kind as to think of allowing me to inflict my company upon her, I should be unable to do so.' There was a surprise in this for him, perhaps for her : pleasure for me to find my nerves my own, and under the government of a Jupiter will in a serene heaven that might have seemed Olympus. She with some few gentle low sentences, bowed to or accepted my words' meaning, and then it was time for her to be going, and I drawing back with an apology to Sir James for being in the way.

Then preliminaries of movement followed by movement, and her (and his) expressions of wish to see me again soon, and she (with him) was away, while I stood bareheaded, watching her as she sat, till the corner was rounded, and she was gone and I alone.

The next morning I found a note from Rayne, asking me to dine with them on Monday. I smiled, and, when I had had breakfast, wrote an answering note of acceptance. Then Strachan came in, and had a short talk with me. He had his doubts about the financial success of the Book, considering that I wished to have illustrations. I was in an absent humour, and simply echoed his remark : yes, I wished it to have illustrations, maps, and everything of that sort.

' Of course,' said he. ' We have abundance of material ; but I am rather inclined to doubt friend Brooke's accuracy in these matters, and, in short . . .'

' Has he taken it ?' asked I. ' Parker, I mean.'

' No :' he said, 'he hasn't taken it—yet ;

but . . . Well, well—we'll talk about that later on. What are you going to do with yourself this morning? A walk; what do you say? I'm just going to the Museum for half an hour or so, to look at some bones Davies has got hold of. Will you come?'

'I'm very sorry,' I said. 'But I do my work in the mornings. I find that if I go out then, it ends in my doing no work at all.'

We made talk of this sort while he was nearing the door and at last had it a little open, when:

'By-the-bye,' I said. 'Did you ever hear of a man called Gwatkin? Sir James Gwatkin, a knight or a baronet, I don't know which.'

'Hum,' he said. 'Gwatkin? Gwatkin? I know the name somehow.— Oh yes, *I* know him! I met him down at Oxford at dinner at a don's—now, two years ago! One of the Culture people. He has written a book about Michaelangelo. I remember him quite well now. The next day I stumbled upon him with Sir Horace Gildea——'

' Horace Gildea ?' said I. ' I was at school with him. Do you know him ?'

The Professor grimaced :

' Yes, a little. He did me the honour of seducing one of my maids.'

I could not help laughing. The Professor proceeded :

' They're an odd lot, those Culture fellows. I don't believe in them myself. A—' (turning his eyes to mine) ' I hope they're not friends of yours, either of these two ? If so, of course I——'

' Nay,' said I, ' they're no friends of mine ! I only wanted to know if you could tell me anything about Sir James Gwatkin —what books he'd written, and that sort of thing. I mean—as I happened to be dining at his house on Monday : one likes to know something about one's host's particular line of thought, if he happens to have one.'

'Ah yes, just so, yes,' said the Professor, turning his eyes to and then away from mine. And on that we parted.

I came back from the closed hall door into the library, and went to the window and stood looking out on the sunny day. A feeling of disgust at work rose in me. I sighed as I took down Antigone, the Greek play I was then reading, and lexicon and translation: and then bundled myself into the easy chair. Folly! and I knew it. None the less I intended proving it once more.

I had last time stopped just before a Chorus. I began on the Chorus now. Such a delightfully corrupt Chorus! and here (in two nice close-printed note columns) was what Hermann thought about the first lines, and then what somebody else thought, and then what the present Editor thought, damn him! Finally I gave it up in disgust: got myself out of the easy chair and the books into it : and stood looking disconsolately into the atmosphere

24—2

of the fine morning. Then the idea of taking a steamer down the fresh breezy river came to me—to Greenwich, and go into the Park, or, first, to see the Painted Chamber, and then for a walk over the heath to look at all the old places. Why not?

I went. It was a fair sweet morning on the river, somehow as I suppose my Italy to be, with the air so pure, like wine that had no fieriness in it. I got out at Greenwich: I saw the old Painted Chamber again, my heart making its flutter felt as I passed along that coloured gallery where I had moved and dreamed in the dimmer air of my boyhood.—Ah, here was Nelson, and here! And here the sacred relics of him. How long, how long ago it was since I stood looking at that pallid body going with its heroic message of, ' *England expects every man to do his duty*,' up to . . . . Where? Somewhere where the pallid bodies of heroes, who have fought the fight and done that duty well, are taken by

soft hands and lain in the quiet of the
Eternal Fields.—And how I used to think
that, in some simple way, although it
seemed so dreamy, that body was *my* body
and that duty well done was *my* duty : and
this small child here, with eyes half-
brimmed with tears, so saw the final
requiem of its own manhood, the seal of
death with which it had sealed life, the
fight well fought, the duty well done, and
the pallid body taken by soft hands and
laid in the quiet of the Eternal Fields.——
' *It is all changed now !'*

I turned from it with the lump of tears
in my throat and went out into the air, and
away, and I thought in this wise : that the
dreams of boyhood are for boyhood and
are dear, while the sights of manhood are
for manhood and are bitter : and, that it
is given to many to desire the well-fought
fight and the well-done duty and the tender
progress to the quiet of the Eternal Fields,
but that few, the dwindling sacred few,
achieve to it : and that it is very hard to

learn this simple lesson, that I, this me, this only real *existence* that I know in space of Time and Life, is one of the many.

As I slowly climbed up the hill, I noted the old tree in the middle of the path, against which I, dizzy and faint from the pernicious tobacco smoke inhaled in the shade of a gnarly oak while the small gentle deer fed round me, leant full of the nausea of this wretchedness, and thought never to incur it again! Then I came in sight of the haunted house, darksome abode of awe and wonder. Then there was the field on the brow of which I had reclined with Wallace, playing some game at ' chuck ' with clasp-knives, looking at times out over the dark, silver-twining Thames, and duskily, far-stretching London ; till one unlucky throw of his spiked my hand (here is the scar on my right thumb still), and how I insisted that there was *not* the end of chuck for the day!

It is all changed now. The field in which we played that game or, lying

along the grass, talked as we ate sugared
compounds or the satisfying parkin. Even
the school is changed. The brass plate is
gone from the gate. The house is freshly
painted and enlarged, but empty. I see
the top of the cherry-tree over the wall.

I turned from it and went down the
little lane, passing many remembered spots
and things, and down the hill and to the
small boat pier. And as I stood I began
to think of my future. There was something of Capua in my present case : not so
much bodily, as spiritual, Capua, and yet I
knew quite well that at the best it was not
in either case a campaigning ground. It
was time I took some steps towards the
great object of supporting myself. *Time!*
more than time! Why had I not thought
of it before? This money of Brooke's—
it was not mine. I had said that I would
not take it : or I had said that I could not
devote myself to the Cause. Oh Jupiter
and the other immortals! I should think
not. . . . And yet, why such a decided

not? Supposing I *did* devote myself.
Well. . . . No, it would not do. 'I don't
care about it. No: I won't do that.
No! I couldn't take and keep the money.
. . . God knows it's a poor earth enough,
this earth: and I don't believe in fire and
brimstone being my reward for doing this
—or any thing. That's nothing. There
is the tribunal of my soul—that ideal of
myself, by which I measure the actual of
myself, and do not care to find too great a
difference between them. It is a poor
earth, this earth ; and it does seem piteous
cruel that I must leave what I love and go
out into the dull world of man to draw in
foul breath and jostle with the crowd for
bread's sake. Perhaps it will be better for
me so.

'And yet,' I thought, standing up at the
bow of the boat and looking across the
river. 'I could wish that I was sleeping
the sleep of death, under the earth: at
rest.'

CHAPTER II.

WHEN I awoke on Monday morning it was into a state of dreaminess: the shadowy realm that is between the night's dreams and the day. Rayne moved in it, with Claire, and now myself; but all so dim and bodiless that they could not be called by names whose counterpart were realities. They were not of the night's dreams: they were not of the day; but emanations. Outside this shadowy realm there was some other emanation, some child's, that was more of the earth than ours that were of this middle place, and it would have entered therein, but could not. So I lay thinking of these things: if thinking is in the realm of thought and no thought, if will and no will. And all the while this child's more-earthly-like emanation would have entered into the shadowy realm and could not. And if this was a distress to any one, I could not tell, not even if it was to myself.—The end was that a start shot up through me, and I awoke to fuller waking. The green blinds covered the two large windows opposite my bed. A little light came in through them and made a submarine atmosphere in the room. This I had known before. I sat up : then raised myself, till I could see myself in the large dressing-table mirror between the two green-blind-covered windows. That made me smile.

After lunch I went out for a walk.

The knowledge that whatever humour I went out in was sure to be different from the humour in which I returned, held to me a momentary trouble now. For I was happy enough with the life of the morning, the mild sunny air and soft heaven, to wish for no better state in which to face the ordeal of to-night. ' Ordeal ? Ay : the

faint tremor that comes to me at the
thought is surely enough to tell me that
to-night *will* be an ordeal. *Ordeal?* No:
what ordeal can there be? Of what am I
thinking? I do not know. Ay: that is
the truth: "I do not know." And yet the
sense of the unknown does not. . . .
What ?—Was ever such confusion? No:
not confusion. What then? I don't
know. It's folly trying to be subtle.' I
gave it up.

That day was a day apart. A day apart
is a day in which the past is pallid: the
present pallid: the future a mist into which
the earth-floor goes, not even unknown: a
days of feelings about feelings, of dreams
about dreams.

I came in from my walk of feelings about
feelings, of dreams about dreams, by about
five. I had seen many things, known
nothing. I realized as I was coming up
the hill that I was hungry. I went to the
top of the kitchen-stairs and called to Mrs.
Herbert, asking if I could have some soup

and rice ? She agreed. I went into the study again, and stood in the window, and looked out.

All at once I drew in a deep sniff, and said aloud :

' You're a damnable fool ! I wonder if a blue pill would do you any good ?'

I sat down in the arm-chair and began to think about things actually. The past came out of its pallidness and took vari-coloured-ness and shapes : the present likewise, with a permeating yellow light. I tried to realize what was meant by ' *I, going to dine at Sir James Gwatkin's, and Rayne.*' Then the soup came in with Mrs. Herbert : and I drank it, and felt better internally. I set to again upon the work of realizing the fact, the meaning of the fact, that ' I was going to dine at Sir James Gwatkin's.' In such hours as this, when one is still in the border-lit mist of the day apart, the difficulty of realizing anything is great. I had only half succeeded by the time the rice came in. I sugared and half-floated it in milk, and began to eat it: the work of realization being consigned for a little to the place of a remand. (It must be remembered that all this was devoid of self-consciousness.) I finished the rice.

Dinner was at seven. I had not the intention of eating a dinner then. It was almost six now by the mantlepiece clock. I got up and rang. Then: 'But Mrs. Herbert,' I thought, ' tells me she has varicose veins.'—Off I went to the top of the kitchen-stairs, and requested a can of hot water.

In a little she brought it up. Then I began slowly to mount the staircase.

As my heavy foot struck the soft carpet, and one or two of the rods sounded, I suddenly recalled my going up the staircase that last night of ours in London. After a few steps, I stopped and looked over the broad banister down upon the dark shiny table where my bed-candle was, and where two had used to be then. Went on again: the thought had occurred to me before this.

But, what *are* such thoughts? Maybe it was that I noticed nothing here then with any endearment: nor do notice anything so now. And yet, I have always supposed that there would be something of . . . of something or other, in living in a house, and alone too, where you had lived with some one that is dead. The sharp sound that struck your hearing would startle you. The lonely depth of the darkness, or the shadowiness, or the gloom would contain its spectre? I cannot say. Death is so dim a thing, if it is anything at all, to me. What do you mean by death? *You* are not dead. *I* am not dead. *Who* is dead?— And with the thought that this was rather ridiculous in me, I came into my bedroom with the hot-water can. The gas was low.

I put down the can on the washing-stand, and went and turned up the gas. The room was all light. I took off my coat and threw it onto the bed.

I washed slowly, thinking, not in an

ordinary way, but also not pallidly, of
general things. There was a little of the
tremulousness in me somewhere, I felt for
a moment vaguely. But I went on thinking as before, and forgot it. I put on,
first one, and then the other dress-boot, with
the small steel shoe-horn, and tied their
laces tight. Then changed my trousers,
and brushed my hair before the mirror.
Then put on my white shirt, and found and
fastened the studs, and my collar to the top
stud. As I was looking for the glass-
topped box that held the white ties, I
thought the gas seemed burning low, and
looked up at it. It was, confound it! I
found the white tie-box in the shadow of the
curtain, and took out a tie, and began to tie
it. My fingers confused. At that instant
everything in me contracted. I stared into
the mirror. *Brooke was looking over my right
shoulder.*

My body was a creeping thrill. I jerked
round like one half-mad, with my fist
tightly clenched, in some way saying :

‘ *Devil !*’

I would have beaten his pale, cold, corpse’s face with my bony fist. There was not anything — except the shadow of, I saw, the bed-top on the upper wall-paper.

I paced up and down the room, looking to right and left.

‘ Assuredly,’ I said aloud in an observer’s way, ‘ I will never believe in ghosts. It is far too easy to see one.’

In a little I came back and finished my hanging tie. I had been startled. There was no mistake about that. If I had really believed that I should have seen him, I pondered, then I *should* have seen him. And yet I desired to strike him. And yet I did not believe in him, someway.

So, having turned down the gas, I came to the staircase-head and began to descend. A certain something, not too far from fear, prompted the idea of a hand reaching onto me from behind. I desired to turn and look. My will overcame my desire. I descended slowly, step after step, in an actor's way rather. My heel sounded on the tesselated floor of the hall. My eye observed of the big clock that it was a quarter to seven. I had beaten that something not too far from fear. I had not looked either round or behind.

I went to the coat-rack, took down my theatre-coat, felt my latch-key in my right pocket, and went to the door. Opened it: went out: and drew it to with a low clang. I left certain things behind in that house —with Mrs. Herbert and her varicose veins !

I laughed as I, walking on, put on the coat, shot open my gibus, and put it on my head. I had been startled. There was no mistake about that. But I was wide awake now, surely. And I was going to dine at Sir James Gwatkin's, and Rayne. I stood on the pavement-edge (in Piccadilly now) and called out:

' Hansom !'

I should be there, with him, with

her in ten minutes—in all human proba-
bility.

The hansom came up, and I got in, and
gave the address—22, Balmoral Street—
up through the opened trap to the man.
We set off quickly, the horse, a small beast,
trotting. When we had gone a little way,
I knocked up at the trap, two or three times
before the man opened it, the horse's speed
slackening.

' Go through the Park,' I said. ' Through
the Park.'

He shut the trap, and the horse's speed
quickened again. The evening was light
and cool, the sun hid behind thick horizon
clouds. We turned through the gates into
the Park. I bent forward a little, looking
at the carriages and people that we passed.

Then we passed by the Marble Arch into
Oxford Street and past the mouth of the
Edgware Road, up which, some way up
which, by a bye-way to the left lay in a
small street, Maitland Street, a small house,
No. 3. She would not be in yet. She

would be still at her work, sitting sewing
probably. Should I ever see her again?
No, best not. Our paths of life went on
in all but opposite directions. Poor child!
' Alone in the world, as if nobody else belonged to her.' Ah me! In a hundred
years, perhaps fifty, perhaps less, it would
all be as if it had never been. And yet I
was not leaving a thing that had to do with
me in a low plain, whereas I was going
away to mount up into a rich bright
country of gentle sunshine? I was going
I knew not where, except that it was into a
dull slate atmosphere like the sky there ;
only that there was no sun, and my feet
scarce held the ground. *' In a hundred
years, it would all be as if it had never been.'*

We drew up sharply. I looked out. It
was the house alright. I threw open the
flaps, and jumped onto the pavement, and
went back and paid the man. Then
ascended the steps, and knocked and rang
as the little brass plate bade : and waited.
A flunky opened the door and ushered me

in. Sir James was coming along the passage parallel to, below the stairs, and saw me. He at once advanced to me, saying cordially :

'Ah, Mr. Leicester, how do you do ?'

We went upstairs together slowly, I just a step behind him : and then through a tall doorway with a deep-red velvet hanging, and along a room that was like a passage : and then he had opened a door and we were together in the soft light of the drawing-room, he just a step behind me.

I at once saw Rayne and some other woman, a young woman, seated close together under the pink-shaded candles, but my look was for Rayne's face, not for her companion's. How beautiful it was ! How steadfast, and how sweet ! And I thought that where I had before seen, as it were, the half-light of her face's form was in the sad wistful face of a child whose body had been sold to an evil task-master—*Claire!* And, at the thought, something of tearful-

ness rose in my heart and gathered to my
eyes ; for that sad wistful child's face had
grown so bright for me and mine so
bright for her, and then we had been parted
by the task-master, who was jealous of the
soul of the body that he had bought, and I
had never seen her again.

'Rayne,' I thought, 'would to God or
Fate or Chance or what it may be, that I
had not found that half-light on *your* face
too. . . . Your hand is soft.'

We had been speaking to one another
with low tones and movements, and now I
was turned from Rayne, bowing to this
young woman her companion, whose name,
his voice had said, was Cholmeley. And
as I looked at her seated there before and
below me, I smiled.

'It is strange,' said I, sinking with the
smile into a chair by her, between her and
Rayne, but nearer to her, 'It is strange
how much men and women have in common. I mean,' I said, leaning on the
elbow next her, and looking at her,

'how much we have in common with one another.'

'Yes?' she said, elevating her brows a little, being a little surprised, I supposed, and wondering what sort of strange masculinity she had come across.

'I mean,' I said, with narrowing eyes, 'that—perhaps no one, can live a life of their own. Suppose a man or a woman give themselves up to (say) love of money, as common a ruling-passion as any other, then that man or that woman will notice, if they only know how to, that their love of money generates, as it were, a subtle odour in their souls, and they will recognise that subtle odour in the souls of others who have given themselves up to the same dominion.'

'Nul de nous n'a l'honneur d'avoir une vie qui soit à lui. Ma vie est la votre,' went on the voice, the voice of him now standing on the end of the hearthrug by Rayne, 'votre vie est la mienne, vous vivez ce que je vis ; la destinée est une.'

'Who says that?' asked I, turning, with the comprehension of it, to him.

'Victor Hugo, in his preface to the "Contemplations."'

'I do not see *how* destiny is one,' said the young woman.

'Here,' said he, 'is the answer for you in eternal words:

'"We are what sun and winds and waters make us."'

'I do not see yet,' she said.

'We are all what we are made. Some of us are made by the sun: and some by the winds: and some by the waters: and some by them all. And that is how, is it not? (as Mr. Leicester has just pointed out,) we have so much in common with one another.'

'And *you* think,' said Rayne to me, with something of a smile, 'that the children of the sun recognise one another accordingly?'

'I suppose I do,' I said, now a little off

the direct scent. 'That is, I think that
any given passion, as a rule, expresses itself
in the same way in different people: and
so one is constantly being struck by resemblances between people, and wondering
wherein these resemblances lie. Am I
clear to you, Miss Cholmeley?' I asked.

'You are too subtle for me,' said the
young woman. 'I am content to do my
duty in that state of life—and the rest:
and leave metaphysics to the choice spirits
like you, and Sir James, and it would
seem you, Rayne.'

But it seemed to me that this young
woman did not, for some reason, care to
have matter of this sort talked now, and
had quietly taken steps to stop it.

We went down to dinner soon after,
Rayne and I, and Sir James and Miss
Cholmeley: we two so far ahead, that I
could say to her in an odd way that I did
not know she had any relation . . . like
Miss Cholmeley.

'Miss Cholmondeley is no relation of

mine,' she said quietly, as we passed through the dining-room door. ' Our names are spelt differently.'

And there the attendant flunkies stood by.

' C-h-o-l-m-o-n-d——,' said I half to myself, the actor's sense growing in me. ' Ah—I beg your pardon !'

The actor's sense went on growing in me as we took our places, and culminated in my high slightly-frowning downward survey of my menu-card : *Soup, Turbot and Lobster Sauce, Quenelles.*—'Damnation !' I said under my breath.

I shivered. And then tightened my jaws, and in an instant thought : ' What foolery is this ? I . . .' I might have been sitting, as I sat in my place that prize-giving day at Whittaker's, waiting for my turn, with my lips rather dry, and every now and then shivering as if a draught came upon me from an opened door. But Blake was *dead.* And Brooke was *dead.* and Mr. Cholmeley was *dead.*—And I raised my eyes and beheld this vision of fair youthfulness; with dark-gold hair whose floating outskirts were sunny, and deep slow eyes, and red lips ripe, and half-transparent teeth-tips, and soft sweet white-ness of the rounded throat whose thought was of the soft sweet white cool body.— There was devilry in it! Up it rose, the unfailing companion, surely for ever the unfailing companion, of my haunting time of inevitable gold-light and mockery that rises. Then it left me, this clearer, dawn-companion : left me to the inevitable gold-light risen mockery, and I could not well know what the voices said in the half-dancing goldy air.

' Is this like the radiations of yellow foaming wine-circles in the brain ?' I thought at last. And all the while they talked, and ate from their plates, and I talked and ate from my plate, and the swift quiet liveried dolls moved hither and thither and bent, ministering to us. One thing was sure, it was a gold-light, half-dancing mockery.

' You do not take wine ?' he was saying.

' Nay,' I was answering, ' I love wine :
wine that is yellow and foaming.'   I could
not, or would not, or did not see any face
but his, bending with a mask's upward smile
to me.

' But you refused to have any champagne
just now ?'

' My dear Lady Gwatkin !' she was saying, the beautiful, voluptuous young woman
was saying (Corisande is her name.   It
sounds like a cleft pomegranate), ' but you
really cannot mean . . .'

' I did not notice it,' I said.   ' I will
have some, if you please.'

And then from a gold-papered bottle-
mouth out came the clear stream into the
large round low glass, all foaming, but
yellow as I lifted it up and drank it.   And
all the while these rings of gold-hued silver
light round my eyes revolved, revolved, revolved outwards : most certainly a gold-
light, half-dancing (half-dancing in the mid

yellow air) mockery. If this was not
devilry, what was? 'It's nonsense,' said
I to myself, ' to tell me that I don't see all
this. I do. It's devilry. The room is
full of the mockery of imps.' I could have
put up my left hand and tried to tear off
this large ring of gold-hued silver light, like
sun's water-reflections on a wall, from
round my eyes, and seen things fitly : I
could have done it, once, twice, three or
four times ; but I did not. I sat there,
filled with the actor's sense, smiling, and
bending and smiling, and smiling and bending and smiling and talking, and, in my
deeper heart, in a sort of way, defied this
devilry. I knew what they were saying, I
knew what I was saying, although I have
forgotten it now. Once, or twice, or three,
or four times, I could have laughed out-
right at all this ; but restrained myself with
the feeling that I did well to restrain myself. I drank more champagne, and then
fell into a somewhat dreamy state, that
made the seeming endless revolution-out-

ward of my eyes' rings fade into a dimmer distance.

They were talking of French literature; a string of names and words scarcely comprehended by me, but there was light laughter in the yellowy air and restrained sadness. There was no one in the room now but us. I was slowly twirling my champagne-glass round, with my eyes on it and a smile; for the light laughter was foaming in the yellowy air, and the sadness almost withdrawn.

Suddenly she, Rayne, rose. I started up. Corisande rose. Then they were moving round the table, and I was with my backward hand on the door-handle, and my face towards her. I had opened the door. She had passed out, lovely Rayne! The young woman was by me, Corisande, the cleft pomegranate, the sweet soft harlot body. I crushed my right hand on the smooth hardness in it. I could have gripped that soft white throat just below the rounded half-shadow of the apple and throttled her;

and, as I cast down the breathless limp
body, softer but less sweet, the harlot body,
been glad with a quiet half-fierce gladness.
I closed to the door softly upon her, and
came back quietly to my place.　Sir James
was looking at something just before and
below his eyes, with the little smile round
the corners of his mouth.　I all but loved
him, for, having a swift thought of that older
'*Arise begone*,' I had another of one sitting
in a summer parlour, with *the fat closing
upon the blade*.　I too had a little smile round
the corners of the mouth.

We talked in a quiet orderly way for a
little ; and then we went upstairs together.

Rayne was seated in her old place on the
sofa, looking half-absently before her ; and
Miss Cholmondeley lying back in the easy
chair in which I had sat.　She stopped
speaking as we came in, looked up at us, or
at Sir James, and smiled slightly.

We talked in low half-nonchalant tones.
The night breeze bulged in the window-
curtain behind Rayne and the sofa with a

slight rustle. There seemed something of hushed, but withal dreamy in the air : perhaps the quiet after the sunny wind tempest of dinner-time.

Then Sir James spoke, his words sounding somewhat as a return to one's past humanity.

' I have as good as promised Mr. Leicester, Corisande,' he said, ' that you would give us Retsky's setting of Vivian's Lullaby. I hope I did not take too much upon myself ?'

She raised her eyebrows a little and the corners of her mouth, as she answered :

' But you forget that I only sang it to you the night before last. Rayne, I am sure, must be heartily tired of the very name of Vivian by this time.'

' No,' she said, ' his story is too sad for one to be so soon tired of hearing his name. I should like to hear the Lullaby again.'

' Vivian,' said Sir James, now addressing me, ' was an old school-fellow of mine, and I might add—friend.'

I asked about Vivian. Sir James gave particulars of him :

'He ran away from Eton and came up to London, with the idea of achieving fame and fortune with his poetry. It is needless to say that he achieved neither. His parents were poor and obstinate—like him, poor fellow! He had the pride of Milton's Satan. He died—starved, rather than ask help from anyone. A volume of his poems has just been published : this is *it*. You were reading it, Rayne ?'

' Yes,' she said : ' I was reading it this morning.'

' How old was he ?' I asked.

' A mere boy,' he said. ' Eighteen or nineteen.—There is nothing very remarkable in any of his poems, as poems. Their chief interest lies in the fact of their having been written by one so young. It is idle to speculate about what he *might* have written if he had lived, but . . . well, one speculates !'

I still stood, thinking.—' Poor fellow ! Nay, but I account him rich ; for the strife of living and the terror of dying are for him both past and over now, and he is at rest.'

Miss Cholmondeley had passed on to the other half of the drawing-room through the hanging lace-curtains, to where Sir James was standing fingering the music. Here was I with my head thrown down like a meditative cow. I made a few steps to by Rayne, and standing before her, with my head half-bent, said something or other purposeless about the Lullaby and Vivian. She answered with something of the same sort. I asked if she liked Retsky's music ? She said she did not much ; but she was afraid she didn't altogether appreciate Retsky. I said that Sir James had been talking about him to me, saying he was the subtlest of modern composers. Doubtless he had written many pieces that were very precious, if not entirely so ? She took no heed of my smile, but said that doubtless that was the reason (his subtleness was the reason) that she did not appreciate him. She only cared for simple music, and

freely admitted that classical music wearied
her. But this Lullaby was not like any
other music of Retsky's that she had heard.
It was simple, and soft and sweet.—I was
about to say that two of these were rather
necessary qualities in a lullaby, especially
if the baby was teething, when a flow of
soft low notes came and made me think
better of it. Certainly Miss Cholmondeley
knew how to play.

I listened attentively. The soft low
notes flowed on, flowed on, flowed on, but
into their softness was gradually growing
a some other sound: more like an invasion
of still dimy water by rolling slaty-
coloured volumes than anything else I
could then think of. I was the song's
now: my whole soul filled with it. A
softer, lower place was heard: softer, far
away from that now gradually fading sound
that was as the rolling slaty-coloured
volumes: lower, closer to the front of the
picture that was in me, the place in which
I felt a presence, two presences were. They

were sleeping : or they were lying together
in rest. Then one of them roused—himself, for it was a man, or a boy with something of a man's soul : roused himself, and
his voice began, at first with unrecognisable
words rolling over the low slaty glassiness
of the water, and rolling about, till that
first melody of soft low flowing notes, all
but filled with the rolling volumes, was
hidden away. And another voice, a woman's,
or a girl's with something of a woman's
soul, answered softly and sweetly. And the
other voice answered softly and deeply, with
the depth of passion. And the rolling,
slaty-coloured volumes of his first unrecognisable words, which had filled the space
between this softer lower place and that first
mingled melody, had filled it into peaceful-
ness, were growing disturbed : the volumed
column of that first mingled melody was
passing down over the slaty glassiness towards this lower place. The voices rose in
an unspeakable harmony together, but some
of it losing itself in the slaty-coloured

rolling volumes that came over the glassiness of the water of the now back-confused picture. And the last line, half-dying, half-fading away, left the whole picture lost in the coloured rolling volumes: from which now came short, sharp notes, like the cracklings of connected and disconnected electric lines: crackle: crackle: crackle. And then the whole thing was whelmed in a full slaty silent flood.

I awoke.

'You remember,' Sir James's voice was saying, 'with what thought Keats closed his sweet, short nightingale's song? that wish to the bright star to be steadfast as *it* was—*not* in lone splendour hung aloft the night and watching the moving waters round earth's human shore or the soft-fallen mask of snow on the mountains and the moors—

> ' " No—yet still steadfast, still unchangeable,
>   pillowed upon my fair Love's ripening breast,
>   to feel for ever its soft fall and swell,
>   awake for ever in a sweet unrest:
>   Still, still to hear her tender-taken breath,
>   and so live ever,—or else swoon to death."

There is just the difference between that
death-song of Vivian's and this of Keats'
that there was between Hylas and Nar-
cissus.'

'Perhaps,' said Miss Cholmondeley, by
him with the music in her hand, and looking at it, 'the difference was between their
deaths rather than their songs. Do you
think *Vivian* would have said : " *Severn—I
—lift me up—I am dying—I shall die easy,
don't be frightened—be firm, and thank God it
has come*"? I don't.'

'No,' said Sir James, 'he would not.
He probably would have died in trying to
lift *himself* up, as Emily Brontë did. But I
was not prepared to have my words pressed
home. I only meant to notice the two
death-songs as being characteristic of the
two singers : the likeness and the difference. Vivian's is a child's dream of a
sensuous death, Keats' a man's. Of course,
any further comparison than the superficial
thoughts suggested by the two death-songs
would be ludicrous.'

'Would it?' asked Miss Cholmondeley, looking up. 'Personally, I prefer Vivian's.'

I suddenly thought she was teasing him. I thought he was mocking Rayne and mocking me; so that that she-devil was as the laughter inside the laughter, the aerial merriment that came from Comus under the low horizon clouds. Her song had bewitched me. I had been arrayed against Rayne a moment ago.—Nay, I cried out to myself, could this be real? Could any human being have gone through what I had this day—in this house? It was a dream. It was a dream. It was a dream. I could not believe. . . . I was bewildered.

I watched Sir James and Miss Cholmondeley cross into the piano-room again, talking, I felt vaguely, about Retsky's conception of the Lullaby. I looked at Rayne. I sat down in the chair I had sat in before going down to dinner. The sensations of being in the chair unsettled my bewilder-

ment.   I spoke, scarcely expecting to hear
my voice's sounds.

'That was a very—marvellous song—
the Lullaby.'

'Yes,' said Rayne, looking at me.

Her look shot through me.   I scarcely
realized what it meant; I only felt it, felt
it, it seemed to me, in every part of my
body and my soul.   A mass of ideas rushed
into my mind.   My eyes flashed.

We spoke some words together.   I do
not know what I said.   I do not think she
knew what she said.   Surely some feeling
was in her, as it was in me?   There was a
sense of mystery in this half-sympathy of
ours.   I went on speaking to her, not knowing what I said (we were in a low soft
melody that rose and fell, and rose and fell.
We were alone.), and not knowing what she
said, or what she thought; but she knew,
not what I said, but what I thought.   My
thoughts grew more distinct:

'Rayne, Rayne, I will not leave you!   I
will rend you from him.   He shall not have

you. Let him have his soft-bodied harlot
there. You are the queen of my soul. Oh,
my queen, my soul, my love, thou art my
hope and strength : in thee have I put my
trust. Rayne !———'

I knew that they were together in the
next room, and that she was playing what
had been that soft melody that rose and fell
and rose and fell. I knew also that they
were absorbed with that now louder melody,
or with it and one another. *We were alone.*
There was something of the villain and his
chance in my heart.—I looked at her. Ay,
she was dazed, a little dazed ; not altogether. But (I looked into my back-
thought again) how could I get her away ?
Get her away ? I clenched my teeth. Take
her by the hand, lead her out, away ! away !
away !

'Rayne !' I said, 'Rayne ! Listen to
me. It is the night of our lives, this. It
is the night of all eternity for us. Come !
quickly !' (She was looking at me with
dilated, almost sightless eyes, opened

breathless mouth, beatless heart : I, too, in
some way. I did not know where we were
—in heaven, in hell, in the earth, with sea
around us, in life, in death, in life-death, in
death-life ; but we were moving, moving
onward, nearing something. For one
moment we, two yet a mingled one, were
together in it, in the centre of Time-Space,
God's—one moment : then gone.) ' *Come !*'
(She had fallen from me and faded into the
air-space. I was alone.)

Then she and I grew, she more quickly,
into ourselves here: and found ourselves
looking at one another.

'Are you ill, Bertram ?' she said.
' What is the matter ?' I half threw
myself back in the chair with something
that partook of smile and laugh and was
neither smile nor laugh. I had been
dreaming again ! She knew nothing ! A
phantasy ! A pure phantasy ! An inner
part of my poor little soul which I had
taken for the centre of Time - Space,
God's !

Then :

‘ Nothing is the matter with me,’ I said ;
‘ now.　I suffer from my eyes occasionally.’　I rose.　‘ Really, Lady Gwatkin, I
am afraid I must be saying good-night,’ I
said.　‘ I——— ’　　I looked　at　her.
‘ Whither away so fast ?’ I thought.　‘ Are
you so sure, oh wiseacre, that she knew,
knows nothing ?　She knew.　She knows.’
Then I thought : ‘ Shall I pass it over in
silence ?　Shall I say anything of sorrow
for it ?　No.　I am not sorry for it.—*My
dream ?　My dream in Paris.’　I rose and
crossed over the stone bridge : came to behind the
carriage and began climbing over it from the
back.　The lady turned and, seeing me, put
out her brown-gloved hand to me : and then
when I would have caught and pressed it
into my bosom, touched my chest with her
finger-tips, the carriage moved. . . .　*For a
moment a superstitious feeling all but
possessed me.　Then I cried to myself
that, at this rate, I might as well become
a clairvoyant, or an augurer, or a fool.—

I looked at her again. (It was not more than four seconds perhaps since I had looked at her before.)

I said :

'I did you wrong. I ask your pardon.'

I left her. I passed across the room and through the door and down, and, as one in a day dream does the things that his body remembers but his soul forgets, took hat and coat and passed out into the night.

I went on.

Then the thought came :

What ? Was it done ? Was it really done ? Was I not in that room with them yet and this was not a dream ?

No, I answered to myself, it was no dream. I had left her. *What did it mean ?* I had left her. I had left her. I had left her. I had left her. I had left her.— Ay : I knew now ! That woman was the woman of my heart and soul. My life had been lived for her since the day I had first dreamt of the dear-girl-comrade. *I had left her.* The cross-road of my heart's life and soul's was reached.—*I had left her.*

I stopped, stopped still: looked inwards.

It was too late!—I had recognised nothing. I had been played with : having been fooled with the phantasy of a free will. *It was too late !* I had been played with.

I went on again.

'The malice of fate is infinite,' I said. ' It is too late.'

And everywhere was dim.

CHAPTER III.

EVERYWHERE was dim. It seemed as if all the rigging of my soul's bark had turned to calcined semblances, that fell, as calcined semblances fall, making no noise. And then it seemed as if some semblance of myself wandered to and fro, and round about, in this strange dim place of noiseless falling calcined semblances, and thought and thought, trying to regain its hue and presence of health, and could not. Snatches of the music of that lifeful past came to me and grew into deeper colour, bringing hope of permanency—only to be lost again in this strange dim place of noiseless falling calcined semblances.

At last the great dim mass was grown pale and receded: my own figure stood darker in the foreground. I began to think. Thought led to criticism of what I had been thinking about. Then, as thinking of the past led to criticism of the past: so criticism of the past led to thinking of the present; and, in the same way, thinking of the present to criticism of it, and criticism of it to thinking of the future. I had vaguely felt in the earlier part of my walk that my body was a little weary: perhaps it was but the action of the mind on it; for, now that the mind was in almost healthy activity again, the body was in sympathy with it. I walked on with a springy step, and began whistling, turning my thought into the parallel though less distinct expression of music.

I had given up Rayne: I mean, my senses did not sympathize with my soul in making her precious to me. I did not altogether recognise this : perhaps I did not care to. I went on, with some enjoyment in the fine clear night, its air and its star-sown heaven, thinking, as I have said, in the two forms of outward and visible whistling and inward and spiritual thought.

I had been in Trafalgar Square, where bells had been ringing and the air filled with an aerial swinging merriment: and the clear-soaring moon up above, and here and there stars. And one particular star twinkling through a slanting downward bank of gauzed clouds.—The memory of this scene that I had half-knowingly absorbed, now came to me as I stood for a moment and looked up at the heaven. I was in that road that I knew so well, that road by which I went to Hampstead. A little higher up on the left hand side was the concrete pillar: the memory of which and its accompaniments made me smile, as, now moving on, I looked to it.

Then I stood looking in the Hampstead pool at innumerous small up-leaping somewhat crescents of moonlight, as from a rain of moonlight only turning to colour as it struck. Sadness came to and grew of me, sadness almost of tears, thoughts of that past that was no more.

I turned and set off homewards. The walking invigorated me, driving away the sadness; but every now and then my new and brighter thoughts were dimmed by some Banquo-like appearance of memoried things that had taken place in Balmoral Street. At last I was foolish enough to bring my will to bear affirmatively upon these troublesome appearances: then unconsciously brought it to bear negatively, and they faded away in a new soft train of thought.

By the time I had got to Dunraven Place, I was almost happy. I let myself in, and entered the library with a light step. The lamp was turned low, casting a tender rose-tinted shadowy light into the air. My supper was laid out, fruits and bread. The scene, colour and scent pleased me. The tender rose-tinted shadowy light, the mellowed silver of the knives and forks, the subdued colour of the rich-bound books and costly ornaments around me. There were two letters on my plate.

'Two letters?' I thought. 'Who the devil should write to *me* ?'

I sat down in the soft chair, reached to some grapes (I was a little hungry), and the plate with the letters on it : put them on the table-cloth just under the lamp, and, eating grapes, observed them.

'One blue, stiff, and with two stamps. A double weight of nonsense probably. The other—oh . . . Rosy. Yes, that's her handwriting. What does the child want? I have not seen her for . . .' (I took up her letter and looked closer at the address.) 'How long? Three weeks? Eh?—Up you go onto the table-cloth ! . . . Good ! Scientific, quite ! Miss Rosebud can wait a little. And now for you, my mystery of blue paper double-stamped. Who the devil are you, and what the devil do you want ? . . . You rip up tenaciously. . . . An en-closure. *Two.* What's this? A cheque-book. Eh? What? And you, oh foreign-papered——' A sudden suspense was in me before I knew of it. I opened the foreign-papered letter of four sheets, and looked at the end of it. '*Colonel James!*' I recognised the writing. I had the other letter open in a moment (from my mother, perhaps! from my father!), and had glanced at it. '*Dead!*' I glanced on :

'. . . Sunday night . . . sympathy . . . last thing . . . spoke . . . name . . . reparat . . . heir . . . in all something more than £1,000 . . . beg to enc . . .'

I looked up.

'Great God,' I thought, 'what's this?'

I read the letter: then re-read it, more slowly. This is what struck me in it. Colonel James had died on Saturday night: had left me his fortune, and a letter —this letter enclosed, about the sending of which to me was almost the last thing he had spoken.

I took up the foreign-papered letter from my knee and began to skim it :

'. . . I have, after some thought, concluded that . . . proper and seemly. . . .
Your mother . . . the regiment stationed
. . . theatre in London . . . against the
advice of all . . . married. [Pause for a
moment. . . . Quartered . . . Cork . . .
unhappiness owing to religious . . . I
. . . and the attentions of a . . . Captain
Melire . . . exchanged . . . Guards . . .
of whom I frequently warned . . . but in
vain . . . shortly ordered to Dungarvan
and subsequently . . . Guernsey. I regret
to have . . . attentions continued, and I
was compelled to speak to your father . . .
neglected warning, and . . . next day
. . . scene with your mother, in which
. . . common talk. I . . . could do no
more, and remained. . . . One night . . .
dining at mess with . . . walked home to-
geth . . . and . . . silence in the house.
She was gone. I could not have imagined
that anything could have made your father,
a man naturally of the most remarkable self-
restraint, and rendered doubly so by his

steadfast relig . . . sat down and cried like a child. I felt that I could not leave him in this condition, and accordingly, after having done all I could to comfort him by religi . . . so completely prostrated by the blow that I began to fear lest . . . sofa; lay there with his face . . . groaning. . . . From that time strange personal dislike to you . . . till at last . . . almost madness . . . considering the state of his health . . . did not, then, think it advisable . . . and as soon as you were able to bear the . . . village in Derby. Most of the rest you know already; for it has been your own life, I mean your education at Mr. Whittaker's and subsequently at Colchester with Dr. Craven. . . . Your father . . . while you were with Mr. Whittaker . . . died . . . Scotland . . . leaving his affairs in a . . . owing to his fatal confidence in. . . . It remains for me only to . . . [' God ! what's this ?'] . . . Late one bleak, windy night last March, about a fortnight after I had . . . you, coming from my club in

Waterloo Place . . . Regent's Street . . . lamp-post . . . unhappy woman pestered me, and . . . [A low cry smothered itself in my throat, my eyes growing to the paper.] I turned, saying, "Here is some money for you. For heaven's sake, go home and . . . on such a night as this . . ." . . . then suddenly caught me by the arm, and cried out: "Captain James, Captain James, don't you know me?—I'm Isabel Leicester." I fell against the lamp-post, and almost . . . The news of her death, the . . . seemed like a horrible dream. At first I could not . . . then she told me that she had accidentally heard from a friend that he was dead, and had . . . and then asked about you. I answered nothing, for reasons which you will, I think, understand. But on her repeating her question, and adding that surely she had a right to know how you were, even if I refused to tell her *where* you were, I felt constrained to speak. I told her that you had been sent, first to a small school, and subsequently to a public school, where you had, I believed, done satisfactorily : and then proceeded to inform her of the events that had led up to your interview with myself three weeks ago, blaming myself as much as I justly considered I could, and you also in the same manner.' [I had made an effort to control my rising feelings, and was forcing myself to read every word.] 'She listened to me very quietly, and, when I had concluded, asked me if I had any idea where you had gone to. I answered that I had none. Then, as she remained silently looking in front of her, and as I began to perceive that any further prolongation of the scene could only be very painful and quite useless to both of us, I . . .' [I suddenly slipped a paragraph, catching only the word 'money.'] '. . . reviled me and flung it into my face with . . . went away. After some moments' thought, I decided that my duty . . . followed her . . . with a policeman I had happened to . . . to an arch under a railway-bridge, where the unhappy creature . . . approached and found that she was sunk in a stupor-like dream . . . and ultimately . . . hospital . . . comforts . . . died.'

Died.

I stood up with the letter in my hanging hand.

Nay, what was the meaning of all this ? —I turned to the table. How many apples were there on that plate ? One, two, three, four, five, six. I rent the letter into pieces.

I strode across the room to the opened window : then looked back sharply, viciously, over my shoulder, almost expecting to see some one, some semi-human figure, with a coll smile on his cold face, behind me. Then the idea of Brooke, come from his grave to mock at me, seemed to cut my brain with a lash of anger's madness. Then it was a loin-swathed, emaciate Christ that stood sardonically there in the shadow. I leaped fiercely to the place, and found that light and shade had tricked me.

Tricked me? Everything had tricked me! I was in a cave of trickery. I cried out:

'Will you tell me that such a combination of circumstances as this could come about without design? O my poor mother, O my poor mother!'

Then the realization of what I had been reading suddenly came to me again, and with it the frantic suspicion of false play: then I began thinking of my mother, taking my sufferings as being the shadow of hers, for she, too, surely had gone through all that I had: then an idea came to me that almost made me shriek out. '*At last, passing somewhat quickly into an alley, I met one face to face under a protruding shadowed lamp. For a moment I stood breathless, with my eyes in the wolfishness and glitter of hers, and then, like a lightning-flash that fills the whole air, terror of her filled me quite. I leaped aside, and then past her, plunged into a dark-covered* way that was behind and beyond her, and hurried on, past. . . .' I began to laugh.

Yes, yes, yes, *I* was the cub of the she-wolf that was driven by hunger into the public way to see what price her empty, filthy carcase would bring! But she found no purchasers. Nor shall I!

Then suddenly:

'Oh, you cursed city!' I cried. 'You furnace-fire, in which life writhes with the corruption of death, you . . . If I could sweep you off the earth with every—God!' I cried, wheeling round convulsively with clenched fists. 'I have a few words to say to you, and then I have done. You have given me sight. I have used it: and it has told me that the earth that you have made and the creatures that you have put into it are foul. You have given me thought: and it has told me, it tells me, that you have no right, be you God a thousand times, to make your creatures foul and then damn them for their foulness:

You have no right to make them foul at
all! You have given me, too, love and
hatred. With the love you have given me,
I loathe you. With the hatred you have
given me, I hate—nay, I despise and scorn
you! I am not even a beggar at your
gate. I am but a worm in the earth that is
but an atom in your universe. But I stand
here and scorn you! Behold, I am in your
hand. You can do with me what you will
—all except this : turn from my heart that
scorn I have of you. Hear my last word
to you, God. It is the last I will ever
speak to you. Henceforth I endure your
acts in silence. If I have joy, I will not
thank you for it. If I have grief, I will
not curse you for it. Henceforth, I am a
stranger to you. If you are, you are to
me as if you were not. If you are
not——' I smiled.

'Enough of this,' I said : 'perhaps something too much. I am sorry I railed. And
yet the poor cuckold that we call soul must
pour forth the lava of its discovered decep-

tion, or it would burst. I have done now, I think.'

I sat down in the chair and straightway began thinking, or trying to think, of what must now be done. In simple words, I had enough money now to live pretty well what life I cared to live.

The effort of will required to break away from the past thought. and make a new present thinking, was greater than seemed at first. I found my thought flowing in two currents at the same time : the upper shallower one of this new present thinking, the lower deeper one of that past thought. I looked up and saw the other letter lying on the table-cloth, where I had thrown it past my plate. This letter was Rosy's. I might as well read it.

I stretched across to it : opened it : and glanced into it :

'. . . I waited for you on Friday night for an hour and a half. And I really did think you would come some time to me, or you would write and tell me why you hadn't come these three Fridays. And I am very sorry if you are angry with me for writing to you to tell you of it; but I think you must have forgotten that you told me that evening that you would come again the next Friday, and I thought perhaps I had made a mistake about it, and that is why I waited these three Fridays, and I think you might have written to tell me why you could not come.

'Minnie is dead. A man hit her across the back with a stick yesterday, Mrs. Smith says, when I was away, and it killed her. I cried about it; which thing I have never had to do before quite like that. Please write to me and explain why you did not come these three Fridays, as you said you would. I hope you will please excuse this long letter and the writing, but I don't suppose you care enough to mind.

'I am,
'Yours truly,
'Rosy Howlet.

'P.S.—I hope you are sorry about Minnie. She was just going to have some kittens, and now I suppose they're all dead too. Is it not dreadful?'

I was smiling. I re-read some parts of it, and then threw it up onto the plate, and rose and began to pace about the room, thinking.

After a time I stopped at the open window.

'"There is a budding morrow in midnight,"' I said.

And then:

'Yes: as well that as anything else.'

And then:

'Perhaps better.'

I took up the lawyer's letter, and having folded, put it on the plate, and Colonel James's letter, and Rosy's, and put the cheque-book on the top. Then, standing thinking, ate all the grapes, and drank a glassful of water, and gathered up what was on the plate, and went upstairs into my room.

The gas was low as I had left it. I turned it up. I set about doing what I intended. I changed my clothes and boots quickly : put the papers I had brought up, together with my usual cheque-book and a pocket-book containing bank-notes to the value of twenty-five pounds, into my breast-coat-pocket, all the gold I had into my right waistcoat-pocket, and all the silver I had into my right trousers'-pocket. I had a sudden thought of packing a portmanteau : or my old black hand-bag. No : I couldn't be troubled with it. I would get what we wanted on the way.

Then I turned out the gas, went down-stairs again, and wrote a short note to Mrs. Herbert, saying what I wished to be done in this matter. And as I sealed up the letter (force of habit, I suppose) I thought that it was lucky Rosy's letter had come in this way. Perhaps I should not have been doing this if it hadn't.

Luck favoured me again : I lit upon a hansom at the end of the street. I told

the man to drive up the Edgware Road,
and I would tell him where to stop.

The gas-lamps burned very faintly.
There was a hush in the place, broken
every now and then by distant sounds of
stirring life. We were going quickly. I
sat thinking.

We were almost at the turning that has
to be taken for Maitland Street. I thrust
my hand out and waved. We came up a
little, as it were, sideways to the pavement.
I got out. How much should I give
the man? I stood with two fingers
in my waistcoat-pocket, thinking of a
sovereign and an order to wait here
for me. Then I determined no: and
took out some silver, and gave him four
shillings.

I went on alone to the corner of the turn
that was to be taken for Maitland Street,
and crossed over into the deeper shadow of
the other side. The horse was wheeling
round: the cab drove away with sounding
hoof-strokes. I went on, but rather slowly.

Then an idea came into my head to run as
far as the corner of Maitland Street.   I set
off.   I knew the place.   I had a thought
of Rosy, passing in front of that fish-shop
and the three flaring gas-jets, with her
bent-down head and hands holding one
another in front.   But there were too
many thoughts of the place, and I thought
them too many times, for them to be anything more than a flight through my tired
brain now, in it and passed away.   I came
to the lamp-post.   I crossed over, and
knocked with strong knuckles at the door.
I dismissed the thought of another knock-
ing of mine at that door.   I waited.   No
sound.   I knocked again as before, but for
longer.   I listened.   No sound.   I knocked
a third time.   Nothing.   This was foolery !
I paused for a moment to think——— About
what ?   Now, if she had only slept in my
room . . . I drew back and looked up.
God ! she did !   That girl, that friend of hers,
don't-know-anything-about-her-history-sir.
I went into the road, and bent down to

pick up something to throw. There was nothing of the sort there.

I gave up an idea of thrusting my finger down between the stone-blocks, to jerk out problematical pebbles, and went into Hill Street, and set about searching for something to throw. I could find nothing. I went on looking in the road, in the hope of seeing a mended place, whence I could take gravel. At last I found one, and found the gravel. Not such bad luck, on the whole. The eternal cussedness of things demanded that I should have wandered a mile or two before I got what I wanted.

I returned. There was no sign of life in the house: no sign of life anywhere here apparently. Her head would be by the left-hand window. I threw up a pebble. It struck a pane: cracked it, I thought, and, falling on the pavement, bounded and rolled into the gutter. I made a step, picked it up, and, standing, threw again. Same result. But I didn't look for the falling pebble: I looked steadily at the window. Surely she was awake.

Now for a little soft earth. Up it went. I looked steadily at the window.

No : nothing.

I sent up some more soft earth, and stood steadily looking at the window.

No—yes. A movement : a movement of the blind. I stepped back, and, taking off my hat, and turning a little sideways, so that she might if possible see something of my face, looked up as before. Another movement of the blind. It was, I thought, drawn aside a little. I held up my outstretched arms.

All at once I knew the blind ran up, heard a hasp strike, and the top half of the window came down. There was something white in the dark space that had been the top half of the window. I cried out with something of a child's exultation :

'Rosy, it's me!—me! Come down and let me in.'

'Good gracious!' said her dear voice,

'how you frightened me! What's the matter?'

'Let me in! let me in! let me in!' I said.

> '" Do thou roll forth a fruit-cake
> out of the rich house,
> and a beaker of wine
> and a basket of cheeses,
> and wheat-bread the swallow
> and the pulse porridge
> does not reject. Say, shall I go away, or something receive?"'

Heaven only knew what the poor child thought of it all! I began laughing at the idea. Then, suddenly serious:

'Mrs. Smith is fast asleep,' I said quietly, 'down here. I want to tell you something—something of the last importance to us both. Will you come and let me in?'

A pause, then:

'Yes,' she said; 'I will come down.'

Then the window was drawn up, and I stood waiting for some minutes. At last I heard her coming down the creaking stairs. A bolt was softly undone at the top of the door, a lock shot back : the door opened in, and I was standing by her in the narrow passage.

'Don't make a noise,' she said, ' or else you'll wake——'

'"The baby?"' I said. She had put on her dress.

She softly closed to the door.

'What's the matter?' she asked. I was struck and pleased by her quiet tone.

'Let's go upstairs,' I said, ' and I'll tell you.'

We went up carefully ; she first, stopping once to tell me to be quiet, or Miss Martin would hear. My fickle thoughts that had become rather pallid (the trouble of going up so carefully, that is so slowly, and the hitting of my head against some damned beam or something), brought me into the shadowy room in no cheerful state. Why had not she lit a light ? She was groping on the mantlepiece for the matches now.

She found them, struck a light; and then there we were in the yellow full glare of the gas for a moment, before she turned it lower. I had not anything to say ready.

At last :

‘ I am too tired,’ I said, ‘ in body and soul to do more than tell you what I want to, simply and shortly. Will you sit down ? there’—(pointing to the foot of the bed), ‘and I will sit here’—(at the head where the bed-clothes were drawn back). The child obeyed in silence. Although I did not look at her, I noticed her : to this extent, that her hair was all disordered, and rather matted, and her cheeks flushed with what I knew was a hot dry flush. I put my hat on the chair by me—the old cane-bottomed chair I knew (the same as of old, save that the hole in its bottom was grown larger). Then I said (she looking at me in a strange way all the time) :

‘ My dear Rosy, I have come to make an offer to you. I have committed a crime here, in London, to-night, which necessitates my bolting out of England at once. I have scarcely any money left — in fact, just

enough to get out of the place with. I
want to know will you come with me?' I
heard her breath go suddenly sharply inwards, and stop for a moment.

Looking at my booted toes shoving together on the carpet, I proceeded:

'I don't know what I'm going to do—supposing I am not caught, that is. But I
dare say I shall be able to turn my hand to
something or other that will do to keep
body and soul together, and I dare say you,
supposing you would care to come with me,
might do the same. It's not a very inviting
prospect to offer anyone—and there's worse
to come yet. I don't believe in marriage.
You would have to come with me as my
mistress. I might tire of you. You would
have no guarantee but my word that I
wouldn't bolt from you there, just as I am
bolting from justice now. You know the
sort of creature I am.' I looked up at her.

Then, in a moment, she was in my arms,
kissing me, laughing, crying, kissing me
over and over again, and I her, speaking

unintelligible sentences, uttering unknown
words. A thrill went through me—the same
thrill, it seemed, that had gone through me
that winter's evening in the farm-house kitchen
where Mary kissed me with her soft red lips,
the same thrill that had gone through me
when I saw Rayne standing there on the sta-
tion platform, while I was carried away from
her. Mary, lifeless mouldered corpse, lying
in the oozy earth : Rayne lost to me for
ever — worse than dead ; they only had
found their ways into this lonely, longing
boy's heart of mine, and she Rosy.

I pressed her closely to me, my cheek
against hers, the tears welling out of my
eyes. The stubborn will seemed broken at
last. But I was tired, tired in body and soul.
Breathless as she was from my embrace, she
yet strained me to her with strength, strained
me to her when my embrace relaxed, held me
when, all things turning and swimming, I
would have fallen. In that place of confused
and dreamy sensations, I felt her hold, and
had some comfort in it. I think I moaned and

muttered things scarcely intelligible to myself. I say, it was the place of confused and
dreamy sensations, but all the while I felt her
hold and had some comfort in it. 'I,' I thought
at last for one moment stationary in mind;
'I, who had never in my life . . .' And I
smiled; for maybe I had felt her hold before, and had some comfort in it. 'The
dear child! the blessed Rosebud! the little
flower!' (Here were the tears again.) 'If
she had said *No*. . . . if I had gone away
without her: what I should have missed!
But I should never have known it.' (I was
becoming conscious through the skin of my
closed lids of the low gas-light) 'I should
have . . .' She was holding me in her
arms: my cheek and the weight of my
head on her breast, and the weight of my
body on hers. I opened my eyes. She
was smiling at me as a new-made mother
might at her wakened child. For a moment
I felt the pleasure of that hold and look.
Then I loosed myself from her and said:

'Damn it, I must have been fainting.'

She nodded her head at me in her old half-merry way.

'That's just what you did, then.'

'My dear child,' I said, getting up to my feet, and making some steps, 'I'm a confounded fool. Let me see. What did I say to you just now?—ah, yes!' wheeling at the door but, feeling a little dizzy somehow, and not desiring that she should be aware of it, came back and sat down on the bed before I said any more.

Then, looking at my booted toes shoving together on the carpet as before, I began :

'We've been making fools of ourselves, especially me—I mean, I. Now listen to me. Did you intend this to mean that you wanted to go with me abroad? Answer me : Yes or no ?'

'Yes,' she said, ' yes!'

'Did you understand what I told you about the crime I'd committed, and the rest of it? Did you understand it, I say— what it *meant ?*'

'I don't mind about it,' she said, ' one

bit, so long as they don't catch you. And
I'm sure they *won't.*'

'How do you know that?'

'It would be so cruel.'

'What would be so cruel?'

'Now that I've got you, for them to
take you straight away from me again.' (I
knew she shook her head.) 'I'm sure they
won't! I'm sure they won't!'

Her tone of voice, almost fierce, made
me smile.

'My dear Rosy,' I said, 'I'm too tired
to spend an hour in asking you to consider
what a serious question all this is. You
must take my words at their full, true
meaning. Do you understand that our life
will be a hard one—perhaps a very hard
one?'

'Yes,' she said; 'I don't mind one bit.'

'Do you understand that I won't marry
you—now or ever?'

No answer.

'Just so,' I said quietly. 'You *didn't*
understand that. You thought I was

joking. I was not. I am not. I am in earnest. I will never marry you, if you come with me : never !'

I rose and stood before her, and looked at her looking fiercely at me.

'Now, my dear child,' I said, 'answer me simply ; but do not hurry. Reflect before you answer. Don't be afraid of saying "No." Believe I shall not break my heart if you say " No." Are you ready to go with a forger, a beggar, an atheist, as his mistress —not as his wife, mind—to a life that must certainly be a hard, perhaps a miserable one ?'

She looked down now, and seemed to be thinking. What of ? *Did* she believe that I wouldn't break my heart if she said 'No'? If that was her thought, I must answer it.

'This very night,' I said, 'I asked another woman to come with me, and she wouldn't. You see the sort of man you have to deal with.'

I waited.

At last :

'Yes,' she said in a low voice, 'I'll go with you.'

'You'll have a hard life of it with me—even supposing the life itself wasn't hard. I mean: you see the sort of man I am. I am a little mad. I care for nobody but myself. Then I'm a terrible liar: you can believe nothing I say. I have told you bushels of lies to-night.'

She rose, and looked me in the face.

'I don't believe you!' she said. 'You're *not* selfish! you're *not* a liar!'

'But I'm quite mad.'

'How can you talk like that?' she cried out pitifully. 'You know I'd go with you wherever you liked in the whole world! You know I would!'

'Very well,' I said, beginning to feel head-confusing effects of this new effort. 'Very well;' and I sat down on the bed almost exhausted.

As I sat with my head bowed, looking at the carpet and not caring to struggle any more, she knelt down in front of me, looking into my face, and then put her arms up and round me. I opened my knees: she put herself between them. I closed my eyes. My head nodded, and nodded, and nodded.

'Ha!' said I, waking with a start, 'what's the time? I mustn't forget to wind up my watch.' I took it out. A quarter-past three. Time had gone quickly.

'Let me see,' I said. 'What time's the morning mail to Paris? . . . Can we get a cab here easily?'

'Yes,' she said, 'there's a mews at the end of the street.'

'It'll be all right if we start by six, I'm sure.' I was thinking what time it was when Brooke and I left Dunraven Place for that train.

The end of it was that I lay down on the bed to rest myself for a few minutes, while she did something or other (I did not notice what she said), and then I fell asleep. Then I was half-awakened by feeling some one bending over me, to kiss me on the lips : to which I objected, and moved my head, but the other lips came after mine, and almost caught them, despite a sharp move back again. I awoke after that: and saw Rosy standing by the door, and the room filled with light not the gaslight.

'Is it time to go ?' I asked.

'Yes,' she said.

I got up.

'Now, what about the cab ? Where is this mews place you told me about, Rosy ?'

'The cab's downstairs at the door waiting.'

'You didn't go and get it, did you ?'

'Yes, I got it.'

A pause. Then :

'What's that ?' I asked, looking at a bundle on the table.

'My things.'

'You needn't take them, you know,' I said.

'But——'

'No; we'll get everything we want in Paris.'

' But——'

' There, now ! there, now !' said I, offering her my arm, and getting her along, expostulating, to the door and opening it. ' Don't talk any more about it ! It's no good talking about it ! Get along with you !'

' But——' she said, turning at the top of the stairs. I put my hand on her mouth, whispering :

' You'll have Miss Martin up in a moment. By-the-bye,' I said, ' do you owe Mrs. Smith anything ?'

' No,' she said. ' *Hush !'*

She went down the dark stairs, I following her. Mrs. Smith was standing by her door. She made a sort of a curtsey to me.

' Good-morning, sir,' she said.

' Good-morning,' I said.

She had the door open for us in a moment. Rosy went out quickly, and was into the cab (a hansom), and I followed, without a further word or sign to the old

devil. As I was getting in, I told the
man, 'Charing Cross,' over the roof, and
then sank down beside her. I bent forward and pulled-to the flaps, and sank
back again with a sigh.

'I have had rather a hard day of it on
the whole,' I said.

'But why did you make me leave——'

I put my hand over her mouth.

'My dear child,' I said, 'I preferred to
let the dead past bury its dead as much as
possible.'

'But——'

I pressed my hand closer.

'And if it's your economical soul that's
alarmed, know, my pippin, that there's no
need for it. I'm not a forger. I'm not a
beggar. I *am* an atheist. I *am* a liar. I
told you that I had told you bushels of lies
to-night, or rather, this morning.' I took
down my hand, adding:

'Now please don't ask more than twenty
questions at a time, and I will do my best
to explain matters.'

I looked at her, seeing her pretty puzzled face, laughed, and gave her a kiss sideways.

'You *are* mad!' she said.

'I am!' I answered. 'Everybody's mad. It's only a question of degree. And the maddest people of all are those that are most sane!'

CHAPTER IV.

FORTUNE favoured our flight. We arrived at Charing Cross in good time for the morning mail. I took two first-class tickets and tipped the guard heavily, and, despite several attempts to break in, successfully, for the privilege of having the compartment to ourselves. I lay back deep in my seat, with my feet up opposite me, full of thought, and almost unobservant of the child, for the first half-hour or so: when I felt her hand steal into mine, and, looking up at her sweet anxious face, smiled, and said:

'Well, Rosy. Here we are, you see!'

'Yes,' she said. 'Here we are.'

My brows came down a little, thoughtfully. Then:

'Are you sorry you came, child?' I asked.

'No, no. Not sorry.'

'Glad then?'

'I would be—if you'd only speak to me.'

I drew down her face and kissed the cheek, and laughed a little.

Then she said:

'What were you thinking about all this long time, that you didn't say anything to me?'

'Well,' I said—'among other things, about where we were to go to.'

'You . . .' she paused.

I proceeded:

'I think the best thing for us to do will be to get out at Calais; not go on to Paris. Suppose we went to some little seaside village in Brittany for a month or so? It must be very hot in Paris now.'

'I will do what you like,' she said.

'Nay; but it ought to be the other way on. Should you like to go to a little seaside village in Brittany for a month or so?'

'Yes,' she answered; 'with you; I have never seen the sea.'

'Very well,' I said; 'we'll get out at Calais.'

We had a beautiful crossing, the sea like a mill-pond. Rosy wasn't sick. Fortune still favoured us, I thought.

At Calais we got out, and I set about making inquiries as to the whereabouts of the desired little seaside village in Brittany. After many difficulties, that ended in—for me at any rate—complete weariness, I found out a place that seemed eligible, Pierlaix.

In Pierlaix we arrived that evening, and found our way to an inn, where we entered, and I demanded two rooms for the night, and something to eat at once. After some trouble, that would have been amusing if it had not been so dreary to us completely wearied out, we were shown two rooms, a bedroom (as we thought) and a sitting-room, which I accepted on the spot, and proceeded to iterate my demands for something to eat and drink at once. (We were in the sitting-room.) They left us.

I opened the folding-windows wide, and stepped out onto the little balcony, into the noise of the sea and the coolness of the evening breeze from over it. As I leant on the rail I felt Rosy at my side, and turned to her. Poor child, how pale and tired she looked!

'Never mind, Rosebud,' said I, putting my arm round her shoulders and smiling at her. 'Keep your heart up! You'll be all right in the morning! I'm afraid the sea disturbed the equanimity of your stomach: What? you don't feel ill?'

'No,' she said; 'I'm all right, thank you.'

'Then let's go up and wash ourselves,' I said. 'I feel very filthy, I don't know what you do.'

We went up into the bedroom together, and made some discoveries regarding the quantity of water here considered sufficient for the ablutions of two. However, this difficulty also was at last overcome; but we gave up the soap in despair. It was just after this that the fat hostess reappeared with considerable complacency, producing a species of scrubbing-brush, as being à coup sûr what monsieur required. (All the English gentlemen had the habit of using it, she explained to the puzzled host beside her.)

When they had gone away :

' I thought you *knew* French,' said Rosy, a little piteously. ' What did she bring that scrubbing-brush up for ?'

Weary and dreary as I was, I exploded into loud laughter at this, and kept on at it till I fell exhausted backward into the bed, and lay. From there, having rested a little while Rosy was trying to wash her face in the bowl that did duty for a basin :

' I was only trying,' I said, ' to make them understand that I should like to have a tub in the morning.'

' I believe the whole hotel was on the

stairs listening,' said Rosy, rather disgustedly. I went off into laughter again.

'I don't see what there's to laugh at,'
she said: which made me continue louder
than before.

She dried her face and hands at the window, with something of dignity in her air—
I suddenly stopped.

'It will be rather fun,' I said, 'seeing
us buying new clothes to-morrow. You
can't expect me to do that for *you*, you
know!'

'*I* shan't,' said she.

'Very well,' I answered philosophically.
'Then . . .' she was crying. I jumped
up and came to her.

'Good gracious child, what's the matter?'
I said, taking her in my arms; I'm
sorry I . . . what is the matter? I hope
I . . .'

'It's very unkind of you,' she sobbed,
'to go on like that at me, and you know
it is.'

'Indeed,' I exclaimed, 'I'm very sorry.

I didn't think you minded my fun, Rosy. I was only joking, you know . . . There, there now! It's all right. Give us a kiss, and let's be friends again.'

'I'm tired,' she said, wiping her eyes: ' and hungry.'

I continued chattering to her, till I at last succeeded in making her quite cheerful, and in that happy humour we went down together into the sitting-room. But, her hunger somewhat appeased by shrimps and fried sand-eels, the tiredness began to acquire the ascendant. Before we were half through dinner, the big brown eyes were blinking fast and frequent, and the little head nodding downwards, and suddenly starting up when it was approaching the table-cloth, at ever shortening intervals. I persuaded her to sit in the arm-chair in front of the window, so that she might look at the sea, since she didn't care to eat any more, while I finished the stewed fruit and three shrivelled apples.

When I had peeled apple number two

and cut it into four pieces, I went round to
have a look at her. She was fast asleep.

I went back and ate the four pieces, and
then apple number three, thinking all the
while about things, till I became quite
dreamy, and, after that, sleepy and very
incoherent in my ideas about things. The
end of this was that I awoke with a start,
and having realized where I was and with
whom, decided that bed was the best place
for both of us. But when I came and
looked at her breathing asleep, so pale and
tired, I did not care to awaken her. And
going, first opened and left open the sitting-
room door, and then the bedroom door, and
returned, intending to carry her up to bed.
The poor child let herself be lifted with no
more trouble than a few uneasy sounds and
movements of her arms; and then up with
her I went, and laid her softly on the bed.
She sighed, and sank into unruffled sleep
again. I made her as comfortable as I
could, and shut the door.

Over the door there was a small window.

The walls of the room were simply boards, polished. I went to the other end, opened the window, and leant out. Below was a garden. I could hear, but not see, the sea. The evening breeze still blew softly and coolly. I gave a large long yawn, and bethought me of sleep. I took off my coat, putting it on the back of a chair, and came and lay down quietly beside the child. I must have fallen asleep almost immediately.

When I awoke, the room was half-full of sunlight, a bird was singing outside, and I saw Rosy, half a yard away, seriously looking at me.

'Good-morning,' I said.

'Good-morning,' she answered.

'. . . I wonder what time it is?'

I got out my watch and looked at it.— Half-past five.

'Stopped,' I said. '. . . How long have you been awake?'

'Oh, a long time.'

'. . . I feel hungry.'

'What time is breakfast going to be?'

'God only knows——or the fat woman. *I* don't know what even the French for it is. Suppose I get up and see.'

I got up; and, feeling very dried and not a little dirty, pulled off my waistcoat and shirt, and entered upon the best course of ablutions possible with the basin and neither sponge nor soap.

'This is certain,' I said, drying myself on the small towel: 'we must have . . . In fact, we must have everything: I never knew what it was to be without a sponge *and* soap before!'

We talked a little about such things, till I was dressed. Then, on my way to go out, I stopped by the bedside, and stooped down over her.

'May I have a kiss?' I asked.

She put her arms up round my neck, and drew me down to her. Our lips would have met, but that I, avoiding hers, kissed her on the cheek. Then I, supporting my-self by my two arms on either side of her (for she still held me), and, looking at her thoughtfully, said :

'If you think you wouldn't be happy with me, my dear Rosy, it is not too late for you to go back again. You know that——'

'Naughty boy !' she said, smiling at me: 'Fancy talking like that !'

'Nay,' I said, 'I was quite serious. You see what a weathercock sort of fool I am: one moment laughing, the next crying, the next cursing. It is not too late to go back again to your old life. Nay, it will never be *too* late. Whenever you are tired of me, you must leave me. Half of what was mine is yours. That goes without the saying. You are your own mistress—now, as always, as far as I am concerned.'

'Very well,' she said. 'Then I'll take you, if you please.'

After a moment :

'That being so,' I said, smiling, 'I am yours—till you are tired of me, that is, and reject me. Till when, I will do my best— what in me lies, that is—to make you happy. So help me my own poor will and love for you !' I bent down and kissed her on the lips.

She seemed to me to understand what I meant.

For the first week or so, there was no one in the inn—or, as they called it, the Hôtel du Midi—but us ; but a good many people came over from the two adjacent towns of St. Denys and Marny to spend the day, going back by the diligence in the evening. Then two Englishmen, evident 'Varsity men or aspirers thereto, en tour, arrived and stayed for a short time ; but, beyond talking with them a little at dinner (what I had taken, by-the-by, for our private sitting-room, turned out to be a public one), we, or rather I, saw nothing of them.

The following, written later on in my last year's autobiography, refers to now :

'I had some things to trouble my peace : to write, and more than once, to Mr. Sandford, the solicitor who had informed me of Colonel James's death and of my inheritance of his fortune, and to Strachan touching the book.

'I scarcely knew what to say to Mr. Sandford. Certainly I was not going to explain to him the cause of my sudden flight, and as certainly I was not going to lie about the matter. In the letter in which he informed me of the burial of Colonel James in Kensal Green, and of the probable cost of a suitable tombstone, etc. : he said that he now regretted, after his long, he might say, personal affection for the deceased, an affection which, etc., and in which, etc., etc., but he must request that I would transfer the conduct of my affairs to, etc., etc., etc.

'I sat frowning over the regular winged writing for a little, with a vague wonder as to the nature of the friendship here alluded to, and sorrow that I had apparently profaned it : then tore the paper across, and threw it on to the table beside me. And Rosy came in with her hat on, ready for a

ramble over the reefs now the tide was out;
and that was the end of the matter—as
regarded the friendship, I mean.

'One afternoon, in a fit of despondency, I
sat down and began a letter to Rayne. I
am not quite sure whether in my inmost
mind I intended absolutely sending it. I
think that the chief reason for my writing, or
rather attempting to write it, was the relief
thereby given to my pent-up feelings.
Sheet after sheet was ripped up, and at
last I sat still in a disgust that was almost
petulant.

'As I sat thinking, a hot flush stole up
to my cheek, and I looked fixedly at the
pile of torn-up paper in front of me, which
contained shameful words : hints, vague
enough, of what I had done. "I could
never see her again," I had said once. "I
could never forget what had passed between
us. How could she expect me to return
and look at her being consumed alive at the
stake of Duty ? No ; I was made of flesh
and blood, and I would I believed in God

that I might thank Him for it! Such a sacrifice as she was making was a sacrifice to Moloch: sin, not heroism."—In any case, how purposeless, all this! in every case, how unmanly! She had to dree her own weird, and I too now, with what light conscience could impart. That was all. All that day I felt I had done a wrong to Rosy. If there was a victim anywhere, it was she.

'Then came Strachan.—I told him simply that it was impossible for me to return to London, at any rate, at present: I hoped never. I was going on to Paris in September, and might perhaps take up my permanent abode there. Could not the proof sheets be sent to me there, and from me on to him? I would write to him again from the Hôtel de Manchester, Rue Faubourg St. Honoré, when I got there. I hoped Parker, Innes, and Co. had accepted the book all right. I should stay at the Hôtel de Manchester till I found a house to please me, I thought. But, more later.

I asked him to excuse haste and confusion.
As a matter of fact, I hated pens, ink, and
paper now. To write at all required an
effort. I was thinking of buying a vine-
yard, and eating fruit till I brought on—
whatever the disease was that was induced
by a surfeit of grapes. I hoped Mrs.
Strachan and the Miss Strachans were well.
It was rather dull weather here. We had
not had a fine summer for long. I doubted
we ever should have one again. And so on.'

A few days after this, a small troop of
students and young ladies who, the fat
hostess assured me, were their brides, arrived, and we had rather noisy times of it
at dinner. Rosy did not like any of them.
They amused me. I used to talk with the
men, or rather boys, as I best could.
(Among other articles purchased by me at
St. Denys, was a French dictionary and a
stock of French novels at which I studied
some hours a day.) But my belief in the
brides (I mean in their brideship) was soon
first considerably shaken, and then alto-

gether demolished. I remember how one
evening I was sitting out on the veranda
(in the evenings the sitting-room was nearly
always deserted for the garden or the country
round about), having been reading the
Mémoires de Jeunes Mariées with some pleasure, when I became aware of one of our
young couples at the bottom of the garden,
sporting together somewhat as I supposed
Isaac to have sported with Rebekah on a
certain historic occasion not unconnected
with Abimelech and a window. The idea
made me laugh, and laugh again, shook
my book down off my knees : when a hand
was put over my eyes and firmly pressed
there. I threw it off, and beheld Rosy
standing absolutely glaring at me.

'Hallo,' I said, 'what's the matter ?'

'You were laughing at one of those girls,'
she said.

'What do you mean ?' I asked. 'I was
laughing at a couple there in the bushes,
playing together.'

'You were *not !* You were laughing at

that girl with the red hair. I saw her go out there a moment ago on purpose to make eyes at you.'

'Are you joking?' I said surprisedly, getting up. I could see she was not. I shrugged my shoulders. She turned, so as to keep her eyes on mine. Our eyes met and stayed together while I spoke:

'My dear Rosy, I do not tell lies, at least of this sort. Once and for all be it understood, that when I tell you I have done a thing, I do not expect you to question—to dream of questioning the truth of my words. Let this be enough. I'm tired of it already.'

'But you *did!*' she burst out. 'You did You know you did!'

'Did what?'

'Nod to her, and laugh at her. I saw you!'

I lost patience and gained what may be called wrath. I gave one step to her, with all that wrath concentrated in my piercing look.

'I warn you never to say such a thing again,' I said. 'If you do, we part. There must be trust between us, or nothing. I did not tell you this before. I thought you understood it. Now choose. Believe me, or we part this moment—for always. I will never see you again.'

If I had not caught her she would have fallen. She writhed about in my grasp, muttering quickly, her face and hands working, her eyelids quivering. I held her and looked at her steadily. I did not know what was the matter with her; but was decided that she must say she believed me, or we would part at once. Life with a woman who did not trust you would be nothing short of the popular conception of hell.

At last she became coherent enough for me to gather that I had terrified her. Then she appeared to recognise me, and covered me with a hundred endearments, beseeching me over and over again not to leave her, or she would kill herself. I did not know how she loved me. Indeed, indeed, she couldn't help it. She always *was* jealous—from a

child. If I would only kiss and be friends
again as we were before, she would never
be jealous again. But that girl with the
red hair *was* so forward-like, she didn't care
what she did !

Weary of this, I sat her down on the sofa,
and stood, half-turned away, before her. She
went on in the same strain for a little, and
then came a pause. Perhaps she was exhausted. I said :

' Well, Rosy, have you considered ? I
was not joking just now. I asked you to
choose. Do you believe what I said to you
about those two down there, or do you not ?
You know what your choice implies ?'

' What ?' she asked ; ' what do you
mean ?'

I patted my foot on the ground to keep
me in patience. I answered :

' I cannot live with anyone who thinks
that I have told a deliberate lie. If you
think I have told *you* a lie, then I will
leave you.'

'I don't think you told a lie. I never said I thought you told a lie.'

'Didn't you say just now you thought I had been "making eyes," as you put it, at that red-haired girl?'

'Yes, I said I thought you did.'

'And didn't I say I had not?'

'Yes.'

'And didn't you say then that I had?'

'Yes.'

'And didn't I assure you that I had not?'

'Yes.'

'And didn't you refuse to believe me?'

'Yes.'

'And what is that but telling me straightly and directly that I had lied to you?'

'I don't understand it,' she said piteously, bewildered. I walked round the table, with my hands in my pockets.

Then, standing in the middle of the open window, I stared out into the dull evening and my thoughts. I do not know how long I stood so: maybe scarcely two minutes, but it seemed more than two hours. I roused

myself with a sigh, turned round, and going
to her, knelt down by her knees, and put
my arms round her, and said :

'My little Rosebud, I'm sorry. I forgot
for a moment that you were so . . so like
a rosebud, and thought (how foolish of
me!) that you were something like a great
big palm tree! I'm sorry. I won't forget
again.'

How the child smiled, and cried, and
laughed, and caressed me !

We came on to Paris in the first week or
so of September, to the Hôtel de Manchester. A letter had arrived there for me
the night before, from Strachan. He ex-
pressed surprise at my flight in the night-
time, and hoped that there was nothing
serious the matter with me. But Mrs.
Strachan had been pestering him to take
her and the girls to Paris for a fortnight,
and as his term at the Queen's College did
not begin till the end of October (by-the-by
he had not informed me that he had just
got the chair of Natural History there, had

he ?), he thought he might manage it (say) half-way through September. We could talk over matters about the book then. Parker had agreed to publish it all right; but there was some lumber about plates, etc. He would write again shortly, or, perhaps better, when he arrived in Paris.

I answered this letter at once.

First, as regarded the book. No expense was to be spared to make it attractive. That was my affair, or rather it was Mr. Brooke's own. I only held his money and property as a guardian till Mr. Starkie returned from Africa, when I should hand it over to him with the account of what had been expended of the one or made use of of the other, during his absence. But, I was quite sure, no possible objection could be raised to any expense undertaken in behalf of the book. I would be responsible for that. For the rest I need not say how glad I should be to see him (Strachan) here in Paris, but it would be, I thought, impossible for me to see Mrs. Strachan or his

daughters. For this reason : there was with
me now one who had given up all she had
for my sake, for which I loved and rever-
enced her, and considering that the only
reason that she was not my wife was because
I did not believe in what was known as
' marriage,' I would go nowhere where she
could not come with me, and be assured of
the same respect as if she *were* my wife.
This I knew was more than I could ask
(my first form of the sentence was : than
either I could ask or desire) of Mrs. Strachan,
with the beliefs that I knew she held. I
repeated that I should be indeed glad to see
him here, I hoped in my own house, and
have some opportunity of returning him
some little of the hospitality which he and
his had given to me while I was in London.

There was, I thought, no more to be
said than this. If he were a true man it
would be enough : if he were not, then let
each go on his separate way. It was as
nothing to me. Only one acquaintance the
less. . . Should I never have a friend ?

In the morning we set out together in pursuit of a house, or rather a flat, to suit us. After some trouble, I remembered that, when I had been at the pension in the Avenue de Fontenoi, I had noticed a flat that was to let, some way up the street, and which had impressed me favourably for some reason or other. I suggested that we should go there now, and we did. The place suited us, and we took it.

We, or rather I, began with a delightful scheme of doing each room (there were seven, not counting the kitchen, all opening into one another) in some particular style : as, for instance, there was to be a terra-cotta room, and a brass room, and a silvered room, and so on. I got through the first two pretty well, I think, but with great trouble, in the next three or four days. Then one morning came a letter from Strachan.—He would manage to see me soon somehow, and we could arrange about the book. He was bound to cross the Channel in any case, he found, before the

term began. There were some bones in the
Museum of Natural History that he must
manage to see somehow before he went on
any further with a monograph on the
Elephas Primogenius he was now working
at. Mrs. Strachan and the girls were not
coming to Paris this year. I must excuse
haste, and, hoping to see me well, he remained, etc.

What a time that was, furnishing the
house and putting my money matters in
order! As for the idea of doing each room
of the house in a particular style—Homme
propose, les commis disposent! I really
don't know how we ever got the place done
at all. However, at the end of a fortnight,
we, or rather I, had made five of the seven
rooms habitable, and the two servants I had
got had done the same for the kitchen. (The
servants of the whole house slept up above
in the grenier, as they call it, not in the
several flats.) I worked like a slave, and
rather liked it: hanging all the pictures,
deciding where, and generally helping, to

put all the things in their places, and so on; for I had my doubts about the Parisian sense of the beautiful in the matter of furniture arrangement.

Rosy's chief anxiety in the matter was as concerned the fate of the things which she had herself ordered, all the linen and the household utensils. She did not care to come up to the place itself, for reasons of her own: not unconnected, I thought, with a small coffin which had happened to be exposed by the door the morning of her first visit, covered with flowers, a child's coffin. Her fear of death was a fear, as far as I could make out, not of death in the abstract but in the concrete : perhaps I should say, she had a fear not of death but of the dead. And yet there must have been some other causes at work ; for when I had asked her, as we went up the staircase, why she hurried by so quickly, she had said in a half-whisper :

'It was a child. Don't let's talk about it.'

It must have been a fine thing in the way of amusement to have seen her ordering her things at the Louvre, her favourite shop, lists in hand. The composition of those lists in the evenings with pen, ink, paper, and dictionary were amusing enough; but she would not hear of my going with her to see their fulfilment.

At last all was ready for her, and the next morning we installed ourselves.

I remember that as we sat together that evening, I looked across to her sitting with far-off eyes with her book, and thought how impossible it was to *know* anything about anyone else. I felt that in her mind a train of ideas existed of which I was absolutely ignorant.

At last:

'Rosy,' I said, getting up, 'I have not welcomed you to your home.'

She rose, and I took her hands, and, looking into her eyes, went on:

'Welcome to it, and may you be happy in it! And here at the beginning of our

new life together, let us say that, whatever
may happen, one thing shall always be
between us—Trust. Believe me,' I said,
taking her in my arms and looking closer
into her eyes. 'Believe me, child, that
without Trust, happiness can never live,
let love be as broad and as deep as is the
sea. My life is yours, almost to make or
mar, and maybe yours is mine. Love, as
I take love to be, the caring for another
more than for yourself,—alas, I have it not
to give you. It is best that I should tell
you this. I do not love you as I should, I
know, to have taken you as I did. That
was the wrong I did you. But I *may* love
you some day; and in the meantime, believe me that all I have to give you, child,
my dearest liking,—I would say love,
knowing that what I mean is of love, but
that I have but just hallowed the word by
its highest flight, and would not now stay
it half-way up.—But do not think that
word of " liking " cold. It is not. Cannot you know this now, as I hold you so,

and look into your eyes? Oh Rosy, give yourself to me, heart and soul! It seems to me as we are now that Love is not so far away from us.'

Her arms pressed me with strange strength. Her face grew to mine. I breathed rather than heard the coming words she said:

'I love you!' thrilling through and through me.

And with the words came something of her soul; for our lips met in a kiss that was her full surrender unto mine: a kiss so sweet, so long, so mingling, that I knew not whether this was death or life, or earth or heaven. And then I thought that it was love.

CHAPTER V.

THE Professor came in upon us after twelve
o'clock lunch, one mild, late October day,
when we were standing together leaning
over the library balcony-rails and watching
the aerial manœuvres of two swifts.

'I am very glad to see you,' I said,
holding his hand and looking into his face.
Then turning to Rosy, who had drawn back
on the sudden appearance of this stranger
by my side, I explained :

'This, my dear, is the friend for whose
sake I wished our house to be in all readiness—Professor Strachan.'

Rosy put out a timid hand, and said
blushingly and softly :

'I am very glad to see you.'

The Professor smiled. Who could help

it ? And then gave an odd glance at me
which I rejected, and that, I think, dismissed some invisible commonplace trouble
of ours into the outer air, and he and I
were in some way more really friends than
we ever had been.

He stayed in Paris for eight or nine
days, during which I had the pleasure of
taking him and the Rosebud to see the three
plays I thought were the best worth seeing.
Those three evenings were quietly happy
ones. He and the child took to one
another, I thought, remarkably: and
therein lay the quiet happiness of those
three evenings to me, to sit still and listen
to their talk, with a certain half-dreaminess
in my thoughts of them, and with a certain
half-wonder in the half-dreaminess—half-
wonder to know this much of the gentle-
ness and tender expansiveness of the man
to the child-girl. I remember how particularly this feeling came into and over me
the last night he was with us, at the Gymnase
it was, and how I thought about it all the

way home, and looking into his eyes as after supper he said good-night to me a second time at the street-door, how the sudden thought came that he knew my thought, and to where did the thought tend ? As I came up the dark staircase with my candle-light sending uncouth shadows about me above and below, I wondered, in a half-vague way, about the meaning of the thing ? And the meaning about this half-vague wondering about the meaning of the thing ? And to where did it all tend ?

When I came into the dining-room, I found Rosy leaning against the mantelpiece warming one foot.

'Are you cold ?' I said, putting down the candle on the table and throwing myself into an easy-chair, with my knuckles up to my mouth and my eyes to her.

'Yes,' she said ; 'I am cold — a little.'

'Why, it's quite warm,' I said.

She made a little motion with her back

expressive of a shiver. I took up a book. She turned her head :

'Don't read any more to night,' she said. 'You're always reading.'

'Am I ?' I asked, looking at the tops of the leaves. 'Perhaps I want to get wise . . . If I were you, I should learn French, Rosy. I'd be only too glad to get you a master. And why not music too ?'

'I don't seem to care about it,' she said.

'You are lazy.'

A pause.

Then I :

'I wish you *would* learn French and music. I am very fond of music.'

She came to me.

'Don't sit on the arm of the chair,' I said, ' or you'll break it.'

She stopped. I continued looking at the tops of the leaves. Then she drew a stool from by the table to by my feet, and sat down upon it and looked at me. In a little I met her gaze.

' Well ?' I said.

' I'll learn the French and the music if you like !' she said.

I laughed.

'Nay, the liking must be yours. I don't want you to do what you don't like.'

' You're always reading,' she said. ' I don't believe you ever think about *me*. You don't care *what* I do—*really*.'

' I don't,' I said quietly. ' You are right.' She seemed struck speechless.

I opened the book and began reading.

At last :

' You don't—care—what—I *do* ?' she repeated in amazement.

' No,' I said. ' You may go the devil as soon as you please. You are a trouble to me.'

Silence. I reading.

At last I said :

' The Professor, you see, came over later than I thought he would.'

A pause.

I felt her hand on my knee.

' Are you joking ?' she said.

' Joking ?' said I, lowering the book and looking at her with surprise. ' Not the least in the world. I said I didn't care what you did. I don't. I've examined myself thoroughly in the matter this last week. I was only waiting till Strachan's visit was over. (By-the-bye, I am going to see him off to-morrow evening.) You remember my agreement with you ? You were to take half my fortune and leave me the moment you tired of me. I have come to the conclusion that it's only fair for me to be able to do the same with you. I'm tired of you. You may go to the devil as soon as you please. We'll arrange business matters later.' I lifted up the book and continued my reading.

In a little she rose and went to the fire-place. I read on. She made no sign of life. A sudden idea came to me that she had fainted—was dead ! I lowered my book : saw her gazing over the table into the air. Got up, throwing the book onto the table by the candle, and said slowly :

'Well, my dear, let's part good friends at the least. It was a blunder on my part, our acquaintance : also . . . a blunder on yours. No ill-feeling on either side ; eh ? In token whereof we will spend one more night together, and then—part ? . . . What ?'

Silence : she still gazing over the table into the air. I advanced, and recognised that I desired her, which made me laugh. It was the first time I had so recognised the fact. She answered nothing : made no motion. A sudden feeling of the cruelty of my experiment seemed to bite me. I had not thought of it in that way : cruelty. I at once began to undo my sewing :

'Well, Rosebud,' said I, taking her two little still hands in mine. 'You little goose, what are you thinking about ?'

At last she looked at me ; looked in my eyes long, till I laughed.

'You are a bad man,' she said.

'You do not mean it?' I said saucily.
'You are a wise woman and—' She had in
a moment, smitten me smartly on the cheek
with the palm of her hand! I burst out
into bright laughter, catching her, as she
sat bolt upright with an expression half-
startled half-defiant, in my arms, and
smothering her cheeks and lips with
kisses . . .

In the end, she was echoing my laughter.
and we were like two half-wild romping
children.

But the experiment was spoilt. Perhaps
it was premature.

I wondered that night, or rather morning.
as I lay awake thinking in the grey light.
while she slept sweetly beside me, why I
had attempted that experiment, and what I
had quite meant by it. And wondering, I
fell asleep.

The next evening, I met the Professor at
the Gare du Nord, as we had arranged, and
(he, at the end of our walk up and down in
the hall, commending Rosy to my care as

a last sudden thought which I felt he hadn't liked to broach as of any other sort) I saw the last of him that was to be seen, and turned away a little sadly.

As I walked home to Rosy, who was waiting for me (to go out a walk she had said, and I had half agreed), I had a half-vague feeling that we two, she and I, were entering upon a somewhat difficult stage of development, and thought of it, as usual, half vaguely. When I opened our door, I found her seated on the ottoman in the hall, dressed in furs, waiting.

'My dear child,' I said, drawing out the latchkey, 'it's quite warm out. How can you expect to walk quickly when you're muffled up like a mummy? and stays on underneath, I'll be bound.' I was smiling. She came towards me with a saucy strut, so to show her small pointed boots. I looked at them and said:

'Oh, frightful!'

She caught me by the arm and half-swung there.

'You're in such a good temper to-day!' she said. 'We'll go to a nice café on the boulevard, and drink café noir, in nice china cups, and play at dominoes. I *do* like dominoes. We will—*Eh?*'

'God help you!' said I. 'You are incorrigible. If you die before me, I will have you buried in stays and patent-leather boots, and have a corset cut on your gravestone. You won't find corsets in heaven when you get there. You will have to migrate further south. There are plenty of them in hell. Satan invented them.'

'How shockingly you do talk!'

'How so? tell me that?' I said seriously.

'You shouldn't talk in that way.'

I sat down laughing on the ottoman.

'Shall we go to the café by the Français?' I said. 'You see, my dear, this earth is, after all, rather an odd place to live in; and we humans—or rather, we beasts—are really, after all, rather odd things to be living in it; and this is all the more so on account of murder and sausages. You might also include prophets and poachers. But, seriously,—shall we go to the café by the Français ?'

'How ridiculous you are!' she said. 'Very well.'

'My dear,' I said, 'shall we take a cab?'

We took a cab, and I talked like a rational (or irrational) being for the rest of the evening.

It was late when we got home again, and the concierge apparently deep in his slumbers; for we stood, I pulling at the bell, Rosy seemingly tired into the quietness of speechless acceptance of things, for over five minutes. At last we got in, and went slowly up the dark staircase together, I thinking of last night's experiment till I began to laugh. Then I found we were standing in front of our own door; perhaps had been standing for some time. Rosy seemed resigned to my apparent eccentricities now. There she stood with her hands muff-wise in her sleeves, and her eyes half closed, and

her little head sleepily quavering downwards.
I chucked her sharply under the chin.

'It's time to get up and eat sally luns,'
I said.

'Good gracious, how you *did* startle me!'
she said. 'What's the matter?'

I drew the latch key out of my pocket,
and, at the first shot, drove it into the key-
hole, and opened in the door. The orna-
mented, luxurious passage looked as it were
warm and almost cosy in the red light of
the hanging oil lamp's little floating redder
core-flame. She went in, and I after her,
closing and locking the door behind me,
while she was on and into the morning-room.
There was a small window halfway up the
left-hand wall of the passage, and it looked
into the library. I could see that the
curtain, that was usually drawn right across
the window, was now only half drawn. I
went and observed what she was doing.
She was on her way across the room—to
the fire, of course. Down she sat on the
hearthrug, and doubtless was staring into

the red-ember realm of castles and strange
forms. Then she looked round: '*Why wasn't
he coming?*' Then back again at the red-
ember realm. What a strange thing for me,
here, in Space and Time and Life, so to be
observing her; here, too, in Space and Time
and Life. What were we to one another?
Not only Rosy to me, and I to Rosy, but
each one of us—each one of us humans to
each other one. The dreamy thought grew
broader in me, my eyes still looking at the
firelight picture there, but not comprehend-
ing it. She looked round again. The movement recalled me to my ordinary self. '*Why
wasn't he coming?*' I felt a sweet tenderness
for the poor child waiting for me there. Oh,
Rosy, Rosy!

Then I was away: through the morning-
room, where, on the sofa, lay her furred coat
and hat, and, parting the curtains of the
doorway, stepped into the library. She was
looking back for me. I threw my hat into
a chair, had off my coat, sent it after the
hat, and came to her. I threw myself down

behind her on the soft hearthrug, and, rest-
ing my head, that was beside her, on my
hand, looking into the eyes that were looking at me :

' Rosy,' I said, ' do you believe in God ?'

' Yes,' she said. And with her eyes in
the red-ember realm, ' of course.'

' Then don't you think you're doing
wrong being with me ?'

' Yes,' she said, with her eyes still in the
red-ember realm.

' And don't you think you'll be punished
for it ?'

' I am sure I shall,' she said.

A pause. I somewhat surprised.

' Then why do you do it ?'

' Because I can't help it.' Her eyes always
in the red-ember realm.

' What do you mean ?'

' I can't help it. Can't you see,' she
said, turning full unfathomed eyes on me,
' I can't help it. I love every muscle in
your body.'

The simplicity of thought, word, voice

made me say, with a suspicion of a small smile round the corners of my mouth: 'That's awkward,' and bring my eyes down to the hearthrug, while I thought for a moment of that last expression of hers and its meaning.

Then, looking up:

'Would you like me to marry you?' I said.

Her eyes went as unfathomed as before into the red-ember realm again, and became distant. Her lips said slowly:

'I *should* like to have you without the sin; but . . . .'

'Well——'

'I shouldn't like you to marry me.'

'Why?'

No answer.

I repeated:

'Why?'

'Can't you see,' she said, turning her eyes to me, but with a more ordinary light in them, '*why* I shouldn't like you to marry me?'

' No,' I said.

She looked to the red-ember realm again, but not into it, and her eyes became dreamy. She would, perhaps, answer me before we were both asleep!

She said : ' I don't think you'd care for me even as much as you do now if you married me. No' (she shook her head), ' I wouldn't like you to marry me. Besides . . . .'

' Well—— ?' I said, in a clear tone, that was meant to show that I really did expect her to satisfy what curiosity I had.

' You will *want* to marry some one,' she said, suddenly looking at me with the more ordinary light in her eyes, ' some day.'

' No,' I said, ' I shall never want to *marry* —*any* one.'

' Ah,' she said, ' wait till you love some one—and then!' She nodded her head.

' Why did you think I didn't marry you ?' I asked.

' Because you didn't want to,' she said.

' No—at least, no to your thought.'

' What do you mean ?'

'I don't believe in marriage. You knew
that. If I did, or had, I would have married
you.'

'That's sinful, not to believe in marriage.
Don't you believe in God?'

'To the best of my belief, no. One thing
I am sure about: I don't believe in Jesus.
I suppose Jesus and God are one and the
same thing to you, are they not?'

'Yes, Jesus is God.'

'And God is Jesus?'

'Yes.'

'How is that?'

'That's the mystery. We don't know.
You ought to have faith, and believe in
it.' I looked down. There was absolutely
no good in attempting to say anything
serious on these matters to her. I felt the
tenderness I had felt for her a little while
ago return to me. I looked up.

'Rosy,' I said, 'I don't like you to think
what I can see you do think about my not
having married you. Will you believe me,
when I tell you that my *dis*belief in Jesus

is quite as strong as your *belief*, and that that, and that only, was the reason why I didn't marry you ? I would not marry any woman in the world, however much I loved her. I could not repeat the words of the marriage service with my lips, and laugh at them in my heart. That would not be true.'

'You would, though,' she said, looking as if with a look of experience at me, who has none, ' if you loved a person.'

What was the good of contradicting her ? I kept silence, with downcast eyes, for a moment : and then asked, I did not care to know why :

'Why, if you believe that you will be punished for all this, don't you ask me to marry you and chance my not caring for you then even as much as I do now—as you say ? What sort of punishment do you think you'll get ?'

'I shall be burned in fire. I knew that long ago. . . . I knew quite well it would be like this some day. I used to pray to

God not to think about you, but I could not help it : I *did* think about you ! When you went away to Paris, I was ill, and I thought I was going to die : and I promised God I would never think about you any more; but I got well again, and I went on thinking about you more than ever ! I couldn't help it. And at last I felt I couldn't do without you. You've no idea what a way I used to get in sometimes. I used to feel as if I must get up that very moment, and go and find you, and hold you in my arms and love you. I couldn't help it. I know I shall be punished for it ; but . . . I can't help it. I suppose I must be.—Then, you see, you came back, and we had those walks together. I knew you didn't care for me ; but you were *so* much to me. I *couldn't* do without you !'

To watch the child as she sat, looking with her half-dreamy, unfathomed eyes into the fire, and to hear her telling her story in this way ! It was pitiful.

I drew myself up beside her, and put my
arm round her shoulders, and leaned her
body against mine. She did not seem to
notice my movement : to feel my arm
round her shoulders. She was silently
looking into the to me unknown place before
her.

'Rosy,' I said, 'Rosebud,' rubbing my
cheek softly against hers, 'I would do anything, if it were only true, to make you
happy. I would marry you to-morrow if it
were not for those . . . those words that
would be so false in my mouth, that I
could not utter them. I could not do that.
But there are, now I think of it, other ways
of marrying people. I will find out about
them. Then, you see, you would be my
wife : I mean, as far as having my name ;
so that no one could think or say anything
against you.' She was shaking her head.
'Nay,' I said, smiling, ' *can't you see* that
in this way you would have a greater, a
more lawful claim, you might say, upon
me, in case I ever *did* want to marry any-

one—with the marriage-service and the rest of it.' I was smiling.

'No,' she said; 'I wouldn't care about that. Not one bit.'

'But suppose,' I said—'suppose I ever *did* fall in love with anyone, and *did* want to marry them ? . . . What then ?'

'Then you'd have to, that's all,' she said.

'But what would you do ?'

'I'd go away, and never see you again.'

'I do hope you wouldn't, Rosy! I hope you never will, whatever comes or goes. You must always be dear to me. You must always let me be your friend.'

'While some other woman *had* you ? That's likely! Oh, *you* don't know what love is !'

'I don't,' I said. 'I was only putting a hypothetical case.—But you know quite well that I never would leave you, however much I loved anyone else.'

'But *I* would leave *you*, if I thought you loved anyone else.'

'But I wouldn't let you know.'

'But you couldn't help it.'

'But I never *shall* love anyone, so——'

'How do you know that? *I* thought *I* never should love anyone; but, you see, I do. I hope you'll love some one some day who doesn't love *you*, and then you'll know what *I* have to suffer.'

A pause.

'Supposing,' said I, 'that I loved you, and you didn't love me.'

'Yes.'

'Well, supposing you loved somebody else, and left me, I shouldn't mind always being your friend.'

She gave a short laugh.

'Wouldn't you! Oh no! I tell you: if I ever found out that you loved any woman besides me! I would go away from you. I would never see you again. You never should have *me* again! The idea of being your —*friend*, as you call it! Do you think I could look at any woman, and know that she had you for her own, and . . . and not *kill* her ?'

She stopped : then began shaking her head and laughing to herself. I eyed her from under gathered brows : I suspected the actor's sense in her as well as in myself. An old, somewhat vague idea, that had been gathered into a cluster of heads, it seemed, a half-century ago, but was really only what might be called last night, now suddenly took a one unmistakable head with two one-seeing eyes that saw one purpose. I turned her head round to me and kissed her full and long on the lips. The effect was strange.—It was a new child this, here with me in a new place of early day's air and light. I could scarce think of the old self of hers that was now gone, gone I knew not where.

'Kiss me again,' she said in a low, half-breathless voice, bringing her mouth towards mine. 'Kiss me.'

A certain devil's light of mirth came into

my eyes. I laughed at her, and drew sharply back with back-spread arms.

'No, no, no,' I said; 'you little green-eyed monster you! You shall chase me for another kiss, if you want it. I . . .' I had stopped.

She bent to me with her hands half-up, frightened a little at the look in my face :

'What is it?' she said. 'What's the matter?'

I leaped up onto my feet. There was devilry in it! Up it rose, the unfailing companion, surely for ever the unfailing companion of my haunting tune of in-evitable gold-light and mockery that rises.

'No,' I said, between my teeth. 'That is foolery! What is the matter with my eyes?'

There was a larger ring of gold-hued silver light, like sun's water-reflections on a wall, round my eyes. I took out my watch. It was ten minutes past one.

She rose and came to me anxiously.

'What is it, dear?' she said. 'Oh, *do*
tell me! What's the matter with you,
dear? Are you ill?'

'Nothing's the matter with me,' I said,
putting my watch into my pocket, 'beyond
that I have something wrong with my eyes.
I will go and see an oculist about it to-
morrow. Now, it's time we were going to
bed. There, there! It's all right, I assure
you. Now, off you go to bed! You're
tired out.'

I took her hand and patted it between my
two: and then led her, with an almost
playful gallantry, to the door-way and held
up one curtain for her to pass. Just
through it, she turned her head and
shoulders back and asked prettily:

'But you will come, too, soon?'

'Yes,' I said, smiling and laughing at
her. 'I have something that I must do,
that will take me a few minutes, and then I
will come.'

I let fall the curtain. In a moment I
heard her step go on.

I took the match-box from the corner of
the mantelpiece and lit two candles, this
seeming endless revolution-outward of my
eyes' ring accompanying my every move.
Then I sat down in the easy-chair and
began to think.—' It was amazing how I
could have been so fooled by such a natural
phenomenon into such a state of (say) superstitious hysteria as I had been by this affection of my eyes. How could I have done it?'

I sat thinking of this for a little, and
then of the events of that night of supreme
folly, or best say madness at once : every
now and then recalled to this physical
revolution outward of my eyes' rings. All
at once it stopped. I took out my watch.
It was half-past one. It had lasted, then,
twenty minutes.

That something which I had said I must
do was now done—done well, as it seemed
to me. That something was the final and
complete clearing away, I thought, of all
the clouding illusion that had blackened the
sight of that strange time of devilry, had

dimmed the sight of the time of acts that had followed upon the other as a summer upon a spring. I was at last free. I saw things as they were, not as they seemed to be. It might well be that illusion would play its part in my future's wilder hours; but it never could be what it had been to the daily hours of my past. *I was free.* And that, I thought, meant something.

I blew out the candles and drew back the hearthrug (for fear of some hot coals falling out of Rosy's especially procured English grate, and burning her and me and the house, and my at last freedom in the night), and then went in to her.

She was already in bed, lying on her side, looking to the door-way curtains; with a deep-shaded candle on the reading-table by the bedside, throwing a light over the lower part of her face, and on one outstretched arm in its long white worked frill, and the hand with upheld fingers on the white rounded edge of the bed. All the rest was shadowed.

'Well ?' I said, smiling, and standing for a moment with the curtains in my backward hands.

She smiled. I crossed over to her, and sat down beside the outstretched arm of the long white worked frill and the hand of the upheld fingers on the white rounded edge of the bed : and took the hand of the upheld fingers, while her two eyes looked quietly in mine : and bent, and softly kissed her two soft red lips : and she softly said :

'You see, I hadn't to chase you for it, after all.'

'No,' I answered. 'I cheerfully do what the dilly-ducks would *not* do : I come to be killed. Death from you is too sweet to be fearful.'

'. . . What do you mean ?'

I kissed her, laughing :

'That I love you.'

'. . . Then I hope you will always mean that ; for I love *you*—oh, I *do* love you, ever so much !'

'More than you love yourself ?'

'I haven't any self to love. It's *all* yours !'

'Then, in loving myself, I shall but be loving you !'

'Yes !'

'And in loving you, I shall but be loving myself ?'

'Yes !'

'Love *must* be unselfish, then, whether it like it or no. For, in loving itself, it only succeeds in loving somebody else. . . . Do you understand it all ?'

And seeing she did not, all of it, I once more bent again, and once more softly kissed her two soft red lips : and she once more softly said :

'I understand *that* part. . . . But I seem to think you might do it over again.'

CHAPTER I.

I HAD accepted something or other that was now the melody of my life : if such a note-less flow of under-music, as of a low silver-shot river in a mist, could be called a melody. I might have called that some-thing or other Fate, or Circumstances, or simply Rosy. I called it nothing at all. It seemed as if I were it, and it me ; or everything it and it everything. The child was, I think, very happy.

I had divided the day off in this way : My books from ten to one ; then lunch ; then generally somewhere with Rosy till four or five ; then two cups of tea and slices of thin bread and butter in the library, with the accompaniment of quiet talk, till talk almost died away in the inspection and desultory reading of desultory books and newspapers; then, at half-past six, dinner; then either somewhere with Rosy again, or a less desultory reading of less desultory books and newspapers till, at ten o'clock, bed. The only real work I did was my morning reading. I devoted three hours each day of the week severally to Homer, Sophocles, Plato, Vergil, Horace, Juvenal, and Dante. I do not think I had any definite aim in view then for this study. I was content to do it, as I did all things, and be still.

Walks with Rosy were not successes at first, for she walked both slowly and badly; but I soon grew accustomed to the slowness, and the badness was remedied by occasional lifts on the way. I liked to listen to her; and she, if she was in good spirits, indulged me to the top of my bent. The childlike and seemingly endless interest that she took in life amused me.

One evening, when we were in her

favourite position—she between my knees talking to me as I sat in the armchair.

'Rosy,' I said, 'I will tell you what you are.'

'Well,' she said, 'what?'

'You are a loving girl. I have not before found the word "love" used in the particular way you use it. So your own word describes you: you are a "loving girl:" one who squeezes softly, and kisses, and tries to steal away breath—in all things soft. I will tell you who was your prototype: a certain Shunamite. "*And let her cherish him and lie in thy bosom.*" And moreover: "*A bundle of myrrh is my well-beloved unto me; he shall lie all night betwixt my breasts.*" And: "*I charge you, O ye daughters of Jerusalem, by the roes and by the hinds of the field, that she stir not up nor awake my love till he pleases.*"'

'Yes,' she said, 'that's me.'

And so it was.

The weather grew colder: bracing and

invigorating to me, enervating to her. At last we had keen frost. She spent most of her time by the fire, generally sitting with her knees gathered up on the hearthrug, reading a book or thinking—heaven knows what about!

My walks were nearly always alone now. Consequently they ceased to be semi-rides and became pure walks. With the pure walks came thought again, to oust its poor substitute of dreamy-way-of-thinking. The frost continued. We had a little snow. At first I tried to get Rosy to take more exercise; but being out of doors in such weather was only misery to her, and so I stopped trying.

'We will go to Italy next winter,' said I one evening, having been for a tramp in the now-falling snow, changed my clothes, and stopped by and above her (she on the hearthrug, that is), with hands alternately patting each other's palms. 'To Italy! to Italy! Italy was the dream of my boyhood. I am a true northman. I have the

migratory instinct in me. Oh Italy,
Italy——'

I stopped, and sat down in the easy-
chair, with hands still alternately patting
each other's palms, and thought about Italy
and my past dream of Italy.

At last :

' You must be very cold,' she said.

' Not I !' I answered, with a sudden look
to her. 'I'm as warm as a toast. By
Jove !' I said, 'I must do something to-
night.' (The something being a something
in my head that seemed to wish for written
expression.) My remark was a sort of
outwork designed to stop any advancing
objections on Rosy's part.

None came. She sat silent on the
hearthrug, with her chin by her up-gathered
knees, and her eyes in the fire. I wished
her away in bed——the best place for her.
I disliked writing with anyone in the room.
As I was settling my desk and writing
materials on the table, I suggested that she
would be better in bed, especially as . . .

'What?' she said, looking round at me.

'You seem so tired,' I said, bringing a chair to my place. 'I wonder you have any marrow left at all, and that your blood's not all curdled or clotted by this time.'

'. . . Is it very cold outside?'

'Very. The snow is all freezing.'

'How long do you think it will last?'

'The snow?'

'No: the cold.—I do hate it so!'

'How can I tell? I . . .' (I had begun writing something) 'don't know.'

'Why do you talk in that way?'

'What way?'

Ultimately Rosy went off to bed, in an injured frame of mind, and I was left alone with my writing. An opening scene of a story had occurred to me, and I was interested in expressing it: a not unfrequent occurrence at that time, so far unfailingly accompanied by gradual loss of interest as the story proceeded till, quite disgusted, I either burnt or cast it into a

MS. drawer of mine, and thought no more of it.

I finished my opening scene in the first heat of emotion, and then, after a pause, re-read what I had written. What seemed to me my grip on, my mastery over the characters I had created, pleased me ; not because it was mine, but because it was there, and in harmony with my mood. Then I sat for long thinking. I began to frame, I framed a resolution in me. There was no need to think, say, or act anything dramatic to be, as it were, a symbol or memoria technica of that resolution. It was early : I was beginning to feel both tiredness and hunger. It was impossible for me, I thought, to sink into mere sensuousness. I had a work to do in the world : I intended to do it. The work would require patient preparation : I was determined that I would give it. I had been unhappy in London : 'Society' was not enough for me. I had been unhappy with Rosy : Love was not enough with me.

I had been unhappy with my dreams: myself was not enough for me. I had lived for 'Society,' for love, for myself, and had found that they did not satisfy me. It was time that I lived for something else—for something higher, and broader, and deeper.

I had realized, or thought that I had realized, that I had a certain work to do in the world, and that if I was, as I had determined I was, to do it, I should have to apply myself to a patient course of preparation. I had spent the three or four days that followed on this determination in the same way outwardly as any other days: that is to say, had done my classical work in the mornings; taken my 'constitutional' in the afternoons; and read in the evenings; but inwardly I had spent these days in a different way from any others of my life. I reviewed my past in order that I might see what causes lay there, that were likely to have an influence on my future. I faced all these causes, good or evil, fearlessly, quietly resolved to encourage those that were good, and do all that lay in me to eradicate those that were evil. The one idea that I kept constantly before me was the idea of Strength : I must be *Strong*.

Rosy looked upon this, my new intercourse with her, with a somewhat suspicious eye. I believe she would far sooner have had the old intercourse with her back again. For, if my caprice leaped in evil-humoured moments far away from her ; so in good-humoured moments it leaped close to her ; whereas, now her line of life and mine seemed, nay, were parallel : now parallel lines are those which are always the same distance from one another, that is to say, that never meet. Rosy, like the true woman she was, was quite ready to offer herself up on the altar of my happiness. It troubled her that now, instead of being, as I ought to have been, capricious, that is to say, selfish, I preserved a uniform cheerfulness of demeanour towards her, was always ready to do her little services, was always ready to prevent her doing me little services. It is true that I had in that happy period of lotus-eating devoted myself to her en bloc ; but, as she had said, or as I had said, in so devoting myself to her en bloc ('loving' was our term) I was but devoting myself to myself en bloc, and vice versa. *Then* all the little services had been hers : I had been capricious ; I had been selfish ; she had delighted in my capriciousness, in my selfishness—whereas, now ! . . . Now I was the highest sinner that is arraigned by Love, the sinless one. What right had *I* to the preserving a uniform cheerfulness of demeanour towards *her?* What right had *I* to the perpetual readiness to do her little services, the perpetual readiness to prevent her doing me little services ? Ah ! thought poor little Rosy, that old time was the better time ; for if it knew the depth of hell, it knew also the height of heaven : whereas, this new time knows only the dead level of purgatory.

I remember how I sat one evening, in

the past dinner-hour when we were together
in the library, observing her and trans-
lating her thoughts into my words, somewhat as above : and how at last, smiling at
her for a dear child, I got up, and went
and chucked her under the chin, and in a
serious way that made her eyes looking at
me brighten up at the anticipation of one of
the old capricious hours, the old capricious
hours so often full of the golden atmosphere
of heaven.   And indeed there was a temptation in the air for me to enjoy one of
those hours again.   Why not ?   I com-
menced.

But it soon made itself apparent to me
that I had set myself, not to be, but to act
Capriciousness.   And yet, I thought in
medias res, it is surely a mistake to suppose
that I have passed quite out of my former
self, as a snake out of its skin, and can no
longer be, but am compelled to act, that
former self ?   No.   It is with the humour
I must quarrel : not the characteristic.
Perhaps the fact of self-consciousness is of

itself quite enough to turn being into acting ?

Ultimately Rosy showed that she too perceived, perhaps more clearly than I gave her credit for, that this was not the doer but rather the actor that was wooing her. She was up and away in a pet: I, tickled by the idea of energetic desire in such a child as the Rosebud, laughing consumedly, and next door to careless about how she took my laughter.—All at once I realized that I had once more been cruel to her: nay, but the word merited to be stronger, brutal. I was serious at once, and away to her to try and soothe her. At last I succeeded.

Rosy's discontent with the new intercourse, as I now called it to myself, seemed to increase. At last I found out that the more cheerful and obliging I was, the more uncheerful and disobliging was she, and this discovery having come to a head during the course of a whole evening, erupted in the bedroom in the shape of

what is usually called a row, reproaches
and tears versus sarcasm and silence. After
a few minutes of Tears, Silence betook
itself out of the bedroom and the house for
a long ramble about the streets, at last
joining itself to Thought in preference to
Irritation, with which it had set out.—I
began to draw a sort of picture of what life
would have been with a woman—like
Rayne, a strong woman. Rayne had, I
felt, been for some time an elevation to me,
and now it seemed that she was growing
into an ideal. After all, was she not the
outward and visible sign of that inward and
spiritual Strength which I worshipped? It
was right that she should become an ideal
to me ; she was a strong woman.

The struggle went on. At times I had
relapses into the old disgust, but, while
there, learnt something about the meaning
of the misery of humanity, and so from evil
drew a certain amount of good. Rosy was
meanwhile apparently in persistent readiness to be suspicious. It occurred to me

once or twice that she thought that there was a woman in the case, and so kept on the look out for proofs. The idea amused me greatly, and once led me to demonstrations of my feeling somewhat in the manner of that chucking under the chin that had been the prelude to my second instance of cruelty, or perhaps brutality to her. She seemed to recognise something ungenuine; for she would have nothing to say to me at that rate, and so I determined to do without the demonstrations in future, and did. I do not know if she was happy at this time. She took a greater interest in her household affairs than before, going out shopping with Amélie in the mornings, drawing up lists of things, and so on. I was pleased to see this; for it gave her something to do.

In this way it came about in a remarkably short time that we two grew more like acquaintances or friends than lovers. Then I realized this, and was rather troubled by it; for I felt that the reason for it was

mine, and that she could not like the present
condition of affairs. But what was to be
done? An inch with a child like Rosy
meant, not an ell, but the whole article.
If I suddenly softened, she would take it as
a sign of repentance, and then—trouble of
all sorts! At present I was working away
at my classics and what composition suggested itself: with occasional fits of disgust, it is true, but avoiding the depths and
getting out of the shallows as soon as
possible. And I bore these occasional fits
with a good deal of philosophy now, as-
cribing them to some internal derangement,
such as of liver, of kidneys, or stomach,
and as such to be endured in patience and
silence. Weather, I found, affected me
considerably.

It was now March, but more like the
traditional May. I took long walks each
day, ten miles as a rule: once out to Père
la Chaise, to look at Brooke's grave with
its '*Thy will be done,*' and saw Balzac's
bust, and De Morny's tomb (De Morny

being a gilded rascal that interested me) and others, and stood and looked thoughtfully over the city that seemed like a great parasite that had driven its claws into the earth. Then there was the Louvre, and the Luxembourg and, sometimes, theatres in the evenings with Rosy. A quietly happy time for me, made happier as the days stole on and found me still unshaken in my scheme of life.

One evening, Rosy having a headache and not caring to go out anywhere, I went for a ramble about the streets, observing the stirring multitude in a most delightfully philosophic way. The conviction of the general poorness of life was the deepest, but quietly deepest, conviction in me. My view of the matter was that, since I was alive and in certain circumstances, the only thing that was to be done was to make the best of it.

The dawn was breaking as I pulled at the concierge's bell. I was a little tired, mentally and bodily. I came upstairs, let

myself in, and went into the study. Not
only the general poorness, but also the
general, and also the particular purposelessness of all life and my life was in me.
I did not care to go to bed, I did not care
to do anything. My eyes fell on my easy-
chair : I went to, and lay back, in it, in a
state that kept, every now and then, rising
to a level, over the edge of which lay
disgust, or may be despair. At last, I rose,
with an impatient curse. Was there *never*
to be an end of this foolery ? Was I
never to have rest, peace, comfort, self-
sufficiency, call it what you please, that
spiritual sailing with spread canvas before
a full and unvarying wind ? *Why* was it ?
Why ? Was it really because the strange
shadow of Purposelessness played the per-
petual-rising Banquo at Life's feast for me ?
Or was it that I was one who could not
lack the Personal Deity with impunity ? I
didn't know, I didn't know ! I wished
that I were dead. I wished that I had
never been born. What Personal Deity

had I *ever* had? What . . . My thoughts stood still. I saw a small child go to the bed and slip down on his knees and tell *Him* about it; but then, remembering that *He* was up in the sky, clasp his two hands together, and look up to *Him*; and say:

'Dear God, You are a long, long way away from me: right up in the deep, blue sky, farther away than even the sun, perhaps, and the moon and the stars.—But I love You! Oh, I love You! because You know everything I think about and everything that I want to do. And I pray that You won't let me die till I am very old and have done all the things I want to do. But please help me to be a great man. Through Jesus Christ our blessèd Lord, Amen.'

I threw up my face with my hands behind my head, and the sob coming to my lips, and the tears to my eyes. 'Oh God, God, why shouldn't I pray now? Is there no one to hear me? Is there no one to—— What? *Rayne!—Rayne! you here!* What?'

Everything in me stood still. She was looking at me through the curtains.

I made a sharp stride and opened them. It was Rosy.

I smiled and then laughed, and—

' You startled me,' I said. ' I took you for a ghost.'

' Took me for a ghost,' she said slowly, advancing slowly, till her eyes were close to mine. I scowled.

' You *called* me Rayne,' she said.

' No :' I said ; ' not you—the ghost.'

Fury seemed suddenly to possess her.

' I hate her !' she cried discordantly.

I took her in my arms, in a half-unconscious way that meant quiet.

' Don't be a fool,' I said. ' Why did you get up ?' She was struggling a little to get free.

I let her go : and turning, walked away to the hearthrug, and stood collecting my thoughts. I felt her hand touch my arm. I looked aside and down, at her face.

'Don't be unkind to me,' she said. 'You're not kind to me!'

'Then,' I said unaffectedly; 'I'm sorry.' I turned again and, putting my hands on her shoulders, looked at her. 'As for that "Don't be a fool," of mine, you mustn't look upon it, or the things I say like it, as unkindness. The words that I say to you are, in reality, said to myself—if not at the time, most certainly afterwards. It is the cursed actor's instinct that makes me say them: that's all. I say them——' The expression of her full, half-dreamy un-fathomed eyes was pleading, pleading all but pitiful. I did not know what to do, what to say.

At last:

'My dear child,' I said seriously; 'I believe you're in love with me.'

She answered nothing.

'I wish you weren't,' I proceeded. 'If you only knew what nonsense it is—love, everything! In ten years, you may be a worm-eaten piece of carrion: in less, perhaps. I too. Where do you think you'll be then ? Where shall *I* be ? What'll be the good of your having loved me ? or of my having loved you ?'

' You don't love me,' she murmured, with eyes now far away.

' By love,' I said, 'I don't know if I love you or not ! Do *you* love *me* ?'

She smiled a little.

' Ah !' said I ; ' I wish to goodness you didn't then !'

' Why shouldn't I if I like ?' she murmured, with her eyes far away and something of the little smile round her lips. I slipped my arm round her shoulders, her cloak-clad shoulders, and led her gently towards the door.

' Come,' I said ; ' we have talked enough. Let us go to bed, and sleep. If so be that——'

Now at the door curtains, I turned a little, saying :

'I have forgotten to blow out the candles.'

I went back and blew them out. She waited for me. We went on together, I with my arm round her shoulders as before, through the dark dining-room, and salon just lit with the light from the open door-frame, and into the lighter morning-room, where I said :

'Are you afraid of death, Rosy ?'

'No,' she said ; 'I'm not afraid of it.'

(We were, through the drawn curtains, in the bedroom lit with two unshaded candles.)

She said no more, nor did I. And we went onto the bed : where I sat her down, and myself close beside her. Her hands she put together in her lap, and her eyes were looking dreamily before her.

'Would you be afraid to die to-night ?' I said softly in her ear—' Rosy.'

'No,' she said.

I showed my teeth, with an upward glance at her.

' *Will* you die to-night ?' I asked, a little evilly.

'What do you mean ?' she said, looking

at me. The same expression was still on my face, nor did I change it.

Will you die with *me* to-night?' I said; ' I am ready to die with *you* : although, my dear, as the saying goes, I don't love you.'

' You are very wicked!' she said, her eyes rounding. ' That would be wrong.'

' No :' (shaking my head down a little) ; ' only tired of it.'

Then I looked at her :

'And so,' I said, ' that would be wrong?'

I took down my hand from her shoulder and stretched out my arms backward and yawned.

' Be it so,' I said; ' that would be wrong.'

I lay awake by her in the dark for a little, thinking about my work, and whether I would go on with it, and whether I would go on with anything. By degrees, my thoughts grew to present occurrences, to to-night's : and then, without thinking whether she was asleep or not, asked— her, I suppose :

' Why did you get up ?'

'Because I wanted to see you.'

I fell into my thoughts again; till at last, 'Ah!' I said to myself, 'if I were but some poor, striving, struggling devil in some country town, and she my brave little wife — some poor, striving, struggling devil of a man of letters, with hopes of some day teaching a callous English society to know him as its " teacher," and she the brave little wife that believed in me! Ah! why have I not had to strive and struggle? Perhaps I should have become a great man some day, then. Life would have been self-sufficing for me. I have almost a mind—a mind to throw away all those disgust-bearing, despair-bearing golden grains, and go out and struggle and strive again. Surely, I was happier as a boy in London than . . .' But there was little good in thinking in this way now, to-night.—I did not ask myself why. I left the thinking and its question alone : and dozed : and fell asleep.

My brain rewarded my mind for its later

thoughts on suicide, by a morning dream.
I was stricken with some disease, the precise nature of which neither I nor anyone
knew. It was at present existing in me
somewhere, dormant. All at once it took
shape in my head and breast. From my
head came a puant reek of bluey corruption,
infinitely foul: in my breast appeared a
fathomless sore, from the crater of which
oozed a sickly, yellowy fluid, infinitely
loathsome. All my body was full of pain,
and the only thing that gave me any relief
was to moan ceaselessly. People stood pityingly around me. I seized pieces of wood
and drove them away. I hated that anyone should hear me moan. But one person
wearilessly returned, till at last I noticed
her body, for it was a naked woman. The
skin of her stomach and ribs was all
shrivelled up and dry; but her breasts
were full and soft and sweet. This I knew;
for I touched and kissed them without
looking at her face, having laid aside my
anger against those who had stood pityingly

around me. At last it struck me that the reason why the skin of her stomach and ribs was all shrivelled up dry was because she had once tight-laced them; and, wondering why her breasts, which I had kissed again, were so full and soft and sweet, I looked up at her face and saw that it was what had once been Rosy's. Then I turned away and stepped over a cliff, and sailed down obliquely towards the rock-foam-line of the quiet sea; but, alighting closer, as a flying duck in the water, in the shingly sand in which I had left a little onward trail, I lay grabbling the shingly sand with my hands to under me; till what had once been Rosy came to me again when, straightway remembering and realizing the infinitely foul reek of my head's recesses and the infinitely loathsome sickly yellow fluid and my fathomless sore, I arose and waded and plunged into the sea which closed over me. But what had once been Rosy was now pursuing me like a sniffing sleuth-hound bitch. The chase was terrific, and the

stench from me spread behind me as I flew
on like the wave-line made by the nose of
a fleet boat in pooly waters. At last I
came upon the ruddy bubbling crater of a
submarine volcano and dived in, she after
me. I felt no heat: only a vague idea that
this now slower chase, this pursuit, had been
enacted before somewhere by some one. We
went on for a long time in the liquid fire at an
equal distance, till, at last, I felt that I was
getting ahead of her. Then I slackened
my speed a little, and the stench from me
grew round me like a cloud. I moved on
again, and began to think that I had desired
to die and could not. I thought this over
and over again, till the desire to die became
almost maddening. In a few moments I
had passed through five things that suffice
to give death, unscathed. I turned and
went through them again, unscathed. Then
it was said to me: '*Jesus Christ says that, un-
less you can die, He will inflict the punishment of
perpetual life-with-death upon you!*' I lifted
up my face frowning and answered: '*If He*

thinks that I would seek death from fear of anything He can do to me, He is mistaken. Here I am, let Him take me.' Then I was taken away to a dim under-world place, and found my arms were round a body, great, naked, flabby, which would come down upon me, and the skin depended a little on the only part I could see of it, the thighs and belly and upper portion of one broad leg. The sweat flowed forth from all my flesh, till the great, naked, flabby body felt steamily wet. Then I perceived that this was my father, as I had held him up before. But I would make no sign of any emotion lest Jesus Christ, who was standing by, should see it. The stench from the recesses of my head and the hollow deep of my breast rose till I was almost suffocated. I knew that Jesus Christ was standing by, there, looking at me, and would make no sign of any emotion. Sulphur rose in my throat : my eyes were suffused with blood: the burthen of the body, the flesh of which was growing round

my arms, pressed heavily upon me. I
knew that if I would I could escape straightway from all these things ; but Jesus Christ
was standing by, there, looking at me and
thinking that I would at last come to Him
and ask Him for *His* death : I made no
sign of any emotion. Then the great,
naked, flabby body began to press down
upon me with a dull, mechanical force, so
that my head was thrust backward, and I
saw that it had a face. At the same time
the dim under-world atmosphere began to
be lit with a certain mild gold radiance, as
of dusky gold shafts through a still, dim
blue water : and I grew to see the features
of the face. The eyes were turned up, so
that only half the pupil was visible : the
round over the cheek-bones was swelled,
and with a little down of hair on the one I
looked at : the mouth, with thick, out-
turned, discoloured lips, gaped. I knew no
more of the face, except that it had some
resemblance to three people that I had
known and one that I had never known till

now. The upward head came slowly down,
as it were, settling upon mine. (I could
not move : I was supporting the body.) It
was not two feet from mine. I felt a slight
breath on some part of my face, not of the
mouth of the thing, but *from* the mouth : I felt
it again and again. The upward head sank
lower : the mouth with the outward-playing
breath was by the top of my hair, by my
eyes that looked into its black inner cave :
the turned-up eyes, the half-visible pupils,
were opposite mine that looked into their
vari-radiated centres (I steadfastly looking,
and, as it were, noticing, so as to master all
expression of any emotion): sank below
mine. Then there was a steadying of itself
in the ever-upward head before it came on.
It came on: the thick out-turned discoloured
lips had pressed mine that did not move. I
felt that something would burst in my brain :
every muscle in me was rigid, the blood in
me was rigid, the thought in me was rigid.
The breath from out of the mouth entered
mine and rolled there in a cloud before de-

scending into me. The face, flabby, clammy, cool, grew to mine. I framed a tremendous curse in my heart, and made a one universal effort to bring it forth—and woke. I was full of many sensations. Rosy's eyes were looking into mine. Not realizing these things, and not unrealizing those things, I said:

'*Thou hast not conquered, Galilean!*'

——I was exhausted, wet with trickling sweat, my mind filled with the images of my dream. I shut my eyes, and, after a little, succeeded in thinking. At last, 'What accursed shadows I saw! Shadows of sin; shadows of a tormented universe. Oh, my God! My time is short. . . . I know it. I shall not get further than Paris. I know it. . . . Blake, old fellow, Allan's dead.— "Dead?" he . . . .'—Poor Brooke! if he had a dream like that 'last night,' no wonder he was 'troubled' with it.

I opened my eyes and looked at Rosy. The idea of her complete unconsciousness of my dream, of the part she had played in it, and of the sort of kiss she had been the means of giving me, struck me as being ludicrous, so that I laughed rather brightly at her. She was a little sleepy, a little languorous, lying with her pretty face deep in the soft pillow, and her escaped hair flowing—brown-gold tresses—round about her head. The sun was on our feet. A little canary she had bought yesterday was singing snatches of song in the morning-room. The idea of her solemn bestowal of that half-awakened kiss made me laugh brightly at her again. The little canary there was singing snatches of song. The sun was on our feet.

CHAPTER II.

THAT evening I received a book and a letter from Mrs. Herbert, enclosing another—from Starkie, at last! I read Mrs. Herbert's first, in order to be able to better give myself up to Starkie's and the book, which I guessed was Brooke's. There was nothing of any interest in hers; a mere report of the satisfactory condition of things at Dunraven Place. Then I opened Starkie's; began reading it slowly. He had caught up Clarkson at Zanzibar. Things were not going as well as they might. Two months frittered away in taking great pains about doing nothing. But they had at last started, and here they were on the Continent. Clarkson wanted to turn down to Lake Intangweolo, instead of making for Lake Eugénie, to explore that block, which was comparatively unknown; whereas the other place was both known and interestless, save for the fact that old Osbaldistone died there. He, Starkie, should like to know what the devil was Clarkson going to do in *that* galère. Catch fever or dysentery and manure the sand? He could not possibly say when they might be back; perhaps not at all. He had a faint hope that it might possibly be before next year was out. But he couldn't write any more of this stuff. He was out of sorts—in the *blues*. Clarkson seemed determined to give his name to a new species of beast, or die in the attempt. They'd do no good this time. Only another instance of wasted time, and wasted treasure, and wasted—life. But here was the end, or he would be tearing up this stuff in disgust.—Mine disgustedly, but truly, OLIVER S. STARKIE.

I began to think about this letter till it struck me that it was odd I had not received it sooner. Then I examined the post-marks,

and found that it had arrived in England
in early February.

'Damn the old woman!' I said, and
pulled the paper covering off what as I had
rightly guessed was Brooke's book, the book.
Rosy asked what was the matter? I explained, and, after a little small talk, took to
examining the book. When I had satisfied
myself, feeling in a sociable humour, I began
talking to Rosy, and she, soon brightening,
came to me gladly. We had a quiet talk
about past things, one of the, if not the,
most quietly pleasureful talks I had ever had
with her. We talked about how she had
made me eat the grapes and had made me
call her Rosy (*Miss* Rosebud, I insisted.
She had not had *all* her own way from the
first!), and how Minnie (poor Minnie!) had
chased the piece of paper under the table :
and how we had gone out for our first walk
together when I was so weak—and stupid
(where was the respectful clerk a good deal
better dressed and, doubtless, fed, than
myself, now?): and how we had tea together

that other evening in my room, with the
fruit and the cakes and all the other things,
including a solemn little owl who wouldn't
laugh properly once the whole time, and the
walk together afterwards. And so on.

And we had in the bedroom a look at a
certain little round silver locket (chosen in
a jeweller's in Edgware Road), of which
there had been some talk in the study, and
I had repeated dramatically :

'But I shall always be able to keep the
locket, you know : and when I look at it I
shall think of you and give a sigh ;' (and I
gave one) ' for—you've been——'

'Don't tease me !' cried Rosy, with
puckered brow and a slap on my arm. And
I didn't.

The next day after breakfast I set upon
my work again, but could make nothing of
it. I felt I had better go out. I went out :
down to the Seine and frittered away half
an hour or so looking at books in the book-
boxes on one of the river walls. It was a
dull grey day, with a certain amount of wind,

east wind I thought: altogether quite like a half-bred London day in early March, before Boreas had grown boisterous.

I lit upon an ill-used copy of a book by an English writer whose name I had heard spoken, evilly spoken, of in my later London days. I was in the humour for buying the book of such a writer, so I bought it and came home with it and straightway began to read it. The subject was an author whom I had been of late accustomed to read both rather frequently and rather carefully. I was struck by the number of my own thoughts that I found. Then there began to creep over me the sense that I had done nothing yet, written nothing yet, that is : a displeasing enough sense when coupled with another that I never should do anything, write anything; anything, at any rate, worth the reading. I envied this man who wrote with such assurance of work done.— About which point Rosy came in from her afternoon walk and we had tea.

It often happened that I was silent at

meals and Rosy content to let me so, I
thought to myself, but this evening, apparently because she saw that I particularly
did not care to talk, she kept on asking me
questions and chattering ceaselessly. For
some time my sense of duty kept successful
guard over my temper and I answered her
quietly; but at last I sent my sense of duty
packing and began to answer her a little
irritably: then, gradually worked into an
aggrieved state by her persistent chatter,
answered her irritably, and at last kept a
frowning silence. She was defiant: went
on chattering and laughing with flushed
cheeks and sparkling eyes, and at last proceeded to tease me. I was not in a humour
to be teased. I said so. She was excited
now and not to be stopped, despite that
Marie was in the room clearing away the
things for dessert. I kept my frowning
silence till Marie was gone, and then said,
as playfully as I could, that I was rather
tired of hearing a certain little tongue wagging
and wished it would stop still for a little.

Then came an indignant flare up, to which I made no answer, not even by looking at anything but the grapes I was eating and my plate : then a second indignant flare up spiced with hot reproaches. I expected wet reproaches to follow : and expected rightly. She was getting tired of them when, having finished my grapes, I got up and went into the study.

I made an attempt to work, but failed : made another attempt, and failed again. I determined I would go out. Then, under the influence of a collapsing sense of tiredness and sleepiness, thought of bed ; but bed meant Rosy, and I could not stand her just at present. I went into the dining-room. She was sitting knitting, or whatever it was, in a chair. I told her that I was going out, and might not be in till late : to which she deigned no answer. I went into the hall and, taking my hat and stick, down and out. Which way to go ? Where to go to ? I stood, beating my trouser-leg with my stick, considering. It was a beautiful night, clear and cool—no moon, with the heavens star-sown.

There was evil in me. I felt it in a little: and did not care to combat it. I walked to the right, a little jerkily. It was not now, Which way to go? but, Where to?

I began to think of piquant pictures of Grévin's—dumpy, strutting little cocottes of undeniable chic, and laughed at the thought. There was evil in me, and I did not care to combat it. Names I knew of the supposed haunts of said dumpy, strutting little cocottes—Rue Blanche 'le Skating Théâtre' (the pronunciation of which, 'le Skatting Théâtre,' made me laugh again), and the Folies Bergère.

I took a cab to the Rue Blanche.

When I entered the hall there was a certain tremulousness in me, chiefly the result of an imperfect sense of wrong-doing, and a little, maybe, of the music and the bright scene. I stalked round the rink, not quite daring to openly regard anyone: in fact, very self-conscious. I sat down at a table, and, having ordered a bock, began to argue with myself for a perfect fool. Here was I, who had pondered on Life and Death and Time and Space and God, absolutely nervous in a hall filled with harlots and harlot-mongers! What more ludicrous? I paid the waiter, drank a little of my bock, and looked about me.

In five or six minutes I was master of myself. In ten I was stalking round the rink, observing the people with interest. I thought I would speak to one of ces dames, and see what she had to say for herself. Variety is pleasing. But ces dames had such uninteresting faces, and such puffed-out breasts and contracted waists, that I found I had no inclination to speak to them. I wandered about for half an hour or so without seeing any face that attracted me; and then went out and (not analysing my motives) took a cab to the Folies Bergere.

At first sight, I liked the place better

than the Rue Blanche : the fountains pleased me, and the seats. Then I was attracted by a vendeuse of somethings or other, who had a finely developed pair of whiskers, quite bushy. I stood and began imagining her point of view of life, till, catching my eye, she smilingly proffered one of her somethings or other, addressing me. This made me laugh, and laughingly declining, pass on. I wandered about. The faces of the women seemed to me a little more interesting than those at the Rue Blanche, but not interesting enough to be spoken to.

Once, coming down a staircase, I found myself faced by myself in a mirror. I paused in my descent for a moment, in which I saw my solemn face set above my shoulders, squared by my hands being clasped together behind my back. The idea of this figure and face stalking about among these people, made me laugh.

At last I grew wearied of it, and went away for a long walk about the streets.

When I came home I found Rosy sitting in the library, in the easy-chair, looking as if she had kept herself awake by means of some sort of emotion : I soon perceived jealousy. In a little she began questioning. Where had I been ? why was I so late ? I answered her simply. First, I had been to the Skating Theatre, in the Rue Blanche, and then to the Folies Bergere : and then for a walk.

Those were bad places : bad women were there ; I needn't have kept her up all this time, and then come and told her that.

How did she mean that I had kept her up ? since when had she taken to sitting up for me when I went out at night ?

She believed that I had been talking with a lot of those women. And why hadn't I gone home with one and never come back here again ? She (Rosy) had always thought it would come to this ! she knew quite well when I went away this evening that I was going after some . . . some one else (tears) : I was a cruel . . .

I thought the child was ill, and tried to comfort her. She would take no comfort. I came to her, intending to try more personal comfort. She was up and, with an intense :

'I *hate* you ! . . . Go away !' herself went away.

After a little pondering, I decided that it would be best to let her alone, and composed myself to sleep in the arm-chair and another chair for my feet.

Marie, entering to dust the room, was apparently the instrument of wakening me from bad dreams. For a little I did not know whether to laugh, or pull a face at myself, or take Rosy's quarrel with me seriously : then, observing the sunshine in the room, determined to go out and get rid of all these spiritual cobwebs. Dried and somewhat dirty as I felt, I would not go into the bedroom and wash myself with the chance of awakening her. I went into the hall and, taking up my stick, onto the landing. I was going down the first flight of steps, with my mind full of thought, when, all at once, there was a stumble, a fall, a clutching at and a missing the bannister, and I was lying, half-stunned and dazed, on the broad step at the foot of the flight.

Then a wrath rose in and burst forth as I rose in a keen :

' B——t !'

This foolery was past all endurance !—I dropped down again : my foot had failed me : the anguish in it, in my ankle particularly, was almost intolerable. I rolled onto my stomach and face, stiffening my muscles so as to bear it without the threatening childish collapse, or, at least, moan. After a little I determined I would get up—up the flight, into the house.

With great pain, aided by my stick, I reached the door, opened it, went in, into the study, and into the easy-chair.

There I began to think. At last I found that I had to wrestle with the old man of the wiry muscles and the hateful breath, the

Natural Supernatural, once more. If I had not wrestled with him, I was quite capable of believing that there was a conspiracy here. I threw him at last, and, having thrown him, felt how much better it would be when my carcase was rotting under the sod and my soul melted in the air, and all these troubles over.

At last Rosy came in, dressed, still in the sulks. I did not speak to her. Wishing I were dead was not the sign of reconciliation or comforting. I was thinking now whether I would send for a doctor for my foot, or no : deciding no. Rosy pretended she had come to look for something, and, not being able to find it, went out again without a word. I could have laughed, but scowled instead.

I got up and made my way to the dining-room doorway, then through the dining-room to the salon doorway. She was in the salon. I had only a moment's hesitation. I crossed half the salon as ordinarily as I could ; but I knew I limped a little,

and this angered. Then I suddenly thought:
Why should I care to disguise from her the
fact that I am hurt ? and limped altogether.
She said nothing. (I noticed by the morning-room clock that it was half-past eight :
she was, as I had supposed, up early.)
In the bedroom, I rang the bell and
went and sat on the bed.

I got my boot off myself, and Amélie,
following my directions, bandaged my ankle
up in a wet napkin. Her final adjusting
touch of the bandage extorted a noise of
some sort from me, and I looked up. Rosy
was standing by the doorway, watching. I
scowled and looked down again. She went
away.

I ordered my breakfast in the study, where
I went, passing by Rosy in the dining-room.
My foot was ceaselessly painful.

I ordered a bed to be put up in what
we called the bath-room for me. Rosy
came into the study at about five, found
a book of hers on the mantlepiece just
above my head, and went out without a

word. I sat thinking, or rather, trying to think.

At half-past Marie brought in the tea, Rosy following her. Then Rosy poured out a cup, put sugar and milk into it, and, taking a piece of cake, retired to the chair in the far-window, where she began to drink the one and eat the other in silence. As I wished for my cup of tea, I got up and poured it out, and, taking a piece of cake, retired to my seat again. I determined that I would have dinner in here, in the shape of some fruit and bread and milk.

When Rosy had done her cup of tea and piece of cake, she renewed them : I, after some thought as to whether the pain of getting them was worth the candle of partaking of them, and the (foolish but natural) display of my feeling toward her in this matter, did not. When she had finished, she put her cup and saucer on the table and went out of the room. I rang and told Marie what I wished about my dinner. I was not angry or even piqued by Rosy's conduct : I was too indifferent to it to be either. The reason why I did not make advances towards reconciliation with her was, that I did not care to trouble myself so far.

During the course of the day Rosy contrived what little annoyances she could for me ; but with no other effect than making me laugh at her simpleness. ' If you quarrel with a woman,' I thought, ' you must expect this sort of thing.'

When I was in bed, I considered what was the real condition of my feelings towards Rosy. Without doubt, they were those of complete indifference, and, perhaps, something more. What had I written even in the lotus-eating time ? ' If to-morrow I were to be transplanted to Egypt or wherever you like, I do not believe that I should be sad, being told that I should not see you again.' And now ?—I ventured to doubt that I was anything but a fool not to myself transplant myself some-where where I could myself tell myself that

I should not see her again. There was no
' imperfect sense of wrong-doing ' in the
thought. It seemed to me to be something little short of folly to stay here and be
troubled with her. I ought to go out into
the world and see its ways, so as to prepare
myself for my work ; that work which was
nothing else than, having by self-culture
and observation got an impression of things
generally, to put down that impression on
paper. Truth was the object of my work,
and, by the very fact that I was a quite un-
prejudiced viewer of the phenomena of what
is called Life, I did not see why I should
not produce such an impression of things
generally ' as posterity should not willingly
let die.' The idea of telling the truth about
things was a pleasing one. I could almost
believe that some day that idea might be of
itself a sufficient incentive to a love of
existence.

CHAPTER III.

Four days passed. Then it seemed to me to be best to put an end to this.

The reconciliation with Rosy was therefore effected, and then there came a flow of gentle tears, soft embracements, and the rest of it: all of which I endured in an actively passive sort of way, as being to the female mind the necessary sequence of a quarrel.

The days sped on again. I was content. Once or twice, I thought to myself that I should, perhaps, have been more content if I had *not* been content; for indifference was to be avoided by me. But there was always the answering thought of this inevitably undecided position of Rosy's and my relation towards one another. One interesting particular I had, as it were, parenthetically learnt from Rosy: that her departure from No. 3 on that memorable evening, with head bent down and hands evidently holding one another in front, was not, as I had supposed, to the streets, but to the house of a Mrs. House, who owed her money for some work she had done. It had been some sign of my philosophy (or indifference) that, on realizing that the whole of this luckless connection of ours rested on a mistake, I had not done more than remark to myself that it was a pity, and, after thinking about it for a few moments, gone on with other thoughts.

One afternoon we were having tea together in the study, both of us reading or skimming illustrated newspapers, when I, hearing a ring at the bell, looked up, and said :

'What's that, I wonder ?'

She suggested that it might be some things which she had got at the Bon Marché in the morning, and proceeded to

explain that she had transferred her custom
from the Louvre to the Bon Marché for
some reason or other which I do not
remember. There came a knock at the
door. She said, 'Entrez!' and Amélie
came in with a letter on the letter-tray
and towards me, saying that it was a letter
for monsieur. I was reflecting that that
knock at the door had struck me as not
being in harmony with the eternal fitness
of things (Marie had, at my request, been
broken of the habit), when Rosy inquired
who had brought it up? As I had my
upward hand on it, Amélie was answering
that it was monsieur the concierge who had
brought it up that very moment, and had
said that he was sorry to have overlooked it
in the morning. A glance at the redirected
address had shown me that it was Rayne's
handwriting. My heart went up to the
bottom of my throat.

'Is it from Professor Strachan?' asked
Rosy as Amélie was going on.

'No,' I said, striving to be full master of myself.

Rosy refrained for further question, and I slowly opened the letter :

'DEAR BERTRAM,

'I should not have written to you, but that many things have come upon me. My little son is dead. God, in His great Love, saw fit to give him to me, as I thought, for my consoling : and He has seen fit, in His great wisdom, to take him away from me again. God's ways are not as our ways.

'I do not say that my affliction is not hard, very, very hard to bear. At times I have doubted that I should ever see the good of it. I do not deny this. But I pray always for Faith in His Goodness, and Faith full and perfect, I am sure, will be given to me before the end. Yes, I am dying ! Perhaps it is better so : and yet, I do not quite mean that. My head, you see, is not quite clear now. There is something I should

like to say to you.   Will you come to me ?
But yet do as you think you ought to, and
remember, that any liking of mine is as
nothing in comparison with your duty.   I
have written too much already.   But you
will understand.   For my head is not clear
now.

'My husband sends this.   He has been
very good to me.   Remember about your
duty.   If I do not see you again, I ask God
to bless and keep you and make you His at
last, as I know He will.'

'Brave heart,' said I to myself—'brave
heart !'

My eyes stayed fixed on her name for a
little : then I thought ; till my thought
from thick shoaledness turned to confusion.

I half crumpled up the letter in my
hands.   Some one touched me on the arm.
I had risen : was standing up, here, in the
room.   It was Rosy.   I did not know she
was here too.

I looked aside at her : her cheeks rosy

red, a star-gleam in her eyes, her brows knit. A vixen.—What did she want?

'It is from her. I know . . . it is from her.—She wants you to go to her?' (She was half-panting out her words.)

'Yes,' I said.

'You will go?'

'Yes.'

'You shall *not* go! Oh, you shall *not* go!—I will not let you go.'

I passed slowly by her upraised hand: then, turning, found her close beside me.

' . . . My dear child . . . she is dying. I must go to her.'

'I will not let you—go!'

'Will not—let me—go?'

I stood, thinking of Rayne.

' . . . Won't you say anything to me?' she cried. 'What does she want with you? What right has she with you? You are not hers!—She wants to take you away from me. I know her.—But she shall not!'

Suddenly she stepped to me and caught me by the arm, crying:

'I *won't* let you go to her ! I *will* not ! you *shall* not go ! I will not *let* you go !'

'Hey ?' I said ; 'what are you talking about ?' And looked at her.

Realizing her to be there, her, the tool Circumstance had chosen to undo me with, the plague of a mistake, her, the red rag flaunted in my face by Circumstance that thought I could not gore horse or man again, I concentrated unutterable hate in my looking at and into her. She shrank back.

'Ah,' she whispered, shivering, 'don't. Don't. Don't. I will let you go. Yes : really, truly, indeed, now, this very moment. Only don't look like that, or I shall shriek.'

I turned away my face again, indifferent : and thought again.

' . . . But you *will* come back ?' pleaded her tearful voice.

'I have told you,' I said. 'Yes.'

'You have told me nothing. Promise me that you will come back. Swear to me that——'

I went to the paper-cupboard, opened it, and stood looking for the time-table. She touched me on the arm. She had come after me. I turned to her and said:

'I tell you that I will come back all right. Now, do not trouble me, Rosy. You see that I am—that I don't want to be troubled.'

'But how long will you be?'

'I can't tell. But not more than a few days: if so much.'

'Oh, what shall I do, what shall I do? You will leave me! And I shall never see you again! You will never be the same to me again.—I *hate* her!'

'My dear child,' I said, 'she is dying. You won't have to hate her long.'

'You love her!'

'I do not.'

'You do, you know you do!' She caught my hand in hers up to her lips. 'I *can't* let you go!' she sobbed.

I comforted her in a quiet way, stroking her hair back:

'Come,' I said, 'don't be silly. Come,
come.' And went on, till all at once it
occurred to me that I ought to have looked
out the time the night mail went, and
paused. The clock struck six.

'By Jove,' I said, half to myself, 'what
a fool I am!' And turned and began rum-
maging in the cupboard till I had found the
time-table. I quickly opened and began
to study it.

A pause.

'I am . . . very sorry,' said her soft
voice by me. 'I didn't mean to vex you.
Will you forgive me?'

'Oh yes, I have nothing to forgive you for.'

'And may I pack your things?'

'You are kind.'

'Don't say that,' she pleaded. 'Will
you give me a kiss, and be friends again?'

I turned round and, with my arm about
her back, gave her a kiss on the cheek. I
was smiling at her child's wobegone face.
Then I plunged into my thoughts again
and, leaving her, went to the window and

at last found out the time of the night-mail. Then I took to walking up and down the room in front of the chimney-piece and fire.

'. . . Will you tell them, please,' I said, 'to be quick with the dinner? I have not much . . . Ah, she is gone.'

I rang the bell and, having turned, saw the envelope of the letter with the papers on the floor at the foot of the easy-chair. I picked it up and considered it. A horrible thought came to me: *Payne might be dead!*

I looked at the postmarks. The letter had taken four days to get to me. I cursed Mrs. Herbert. Where was the letter?

I found it in my waistcoat pocket, put there I did not know when.

Marie opened the door. I told her to tell Amélie to be as quick with dinner as possible, as I wanted to catch a train. Marie agreed and went back, closing the door.

'I have found your small portman-

teau,' said Rosy, coming into the dining-
room doorway with a noise of the curtain-
rings. 'Will you come and choose the
things you want, because I'm not sure?'

We went together.

When we, or more particularly I, had
finished packing the portmanteau, we went
in to dinner. The portmanteau was to be
taken down the back staircase. Neither
Rosy nor I could eat much. I was thinking of Rayne.

After what must have been a rather long
silence :

'I forgot the flask,' she said. 'Do you
know where it is? You'd like to take the
flask with some brandy in it? It's such a
pretty flask, and you've never used it.' (She
had given it me.)

'Yes,' I said; 'oh, to be sure.' And
told Marie to go and bring it.

Marie brought it, and then came the
question of the brandy. There was none
in the house : which had not struck any of
us before. I was for not minding about it,

till I saw that Rosy would be hurt if her flask was not used: so Marie was sent out to get some brandy, while Rosy and I went into the study again, not caring for more dinner. There I sat down in the easy-chair, with full thought, and Rosy quietly brought a chair to by mine and sat down and took my hand from my knee to within hers on her lap. So we sat in silence.

Then Marie returned with the flask filled, which Rosy took from me, and reaching, put on the table. It was not yet time to start. We sat in silence, as before; till my thought was less full and I turned my head to look at her with large upward eyes whose gaze was far away somewhere.

'Are you all right now?' I asked.

'Yes,' she said, 'I am all right.'

I was sorry for her: somehow as I had been sorry for her sitting on the hearth-rug in the fire-lit room waiting for me who stood at that small window there. I could not help thinking of the exceeding pity of it, that that mistake had been made, to give

me to her—and her to me. I began to
consider that, it could not always be an
inevitably undecided position, Rosy's and
my relations towards one another. Here
we were : what were we to do ?

I put my arm round her neck and drew
her cheek to meet my lips :

'Poor little Rosebud,' I said. 'Poor
little Rosebud !'

Then I felt the tears coming soft from her
eyes : and the memory of a scene rose before me, when I said :

'Why, little Rosebud. You mustn't mind
like that, you know. I'll come back again
some day—quite soon.'

Ah, I *had* come back again, and had
brought her, not a bonnet with blue rib-
bons and a flower that should look so real
that the butterflies should settle on it, but
what she wanted—myself : and what I had
promised with myself, some grapes and
bon-bons : and, what I had not promised
with myself, some thorns and nettles. Alas,
alas, alas ! And it *was* alas, for she was

indeed alone in the world, quite alone, as
if nobody else belonged to her. . . .
'*Good-night, Rosebud.   Good-night!*'

Well, there was no good in this.

I said :

> '"The cocks they crew, and the horns blew,
>   And the lions took the hill ;
> And Willie he gaed hame again,
>   To his hard task and till."

—I must be off, my pippin, or I shall
miss the train.'   And got up and went
across the room and turned, looking at
her.

She rose and, saying : ' I will fetch your
coat,' went out through the doorway, leaving me with my mental stretching and
rubbing of limbs that had been asleep and
wakened up to the feeling that their blood
was sluggish.

Presently she returned with my great-
coat, which I took with thanks from her,
and then I felt that she felt that the final
embrace was coming.   In a moment it was
come.   She was in my arms, pressing up

with a poor little tearful face for the soft
lips' kiss. None other kiss than that now,
somehow : none other kiss than that now.
Oh Rosebud, Rosebud, all thy poor pitiful
little love is poured forth in it : oh Rosebud,
Rosebud, wherefore not content to be still and
let him pass from thee, rather than to drain
the cup to the lees ? But so it was, and
so I gave it. Then our beings, scarce met,
parted again : and I had left her.

I picked up my hat from the stand, and
was pacing to the door, when the thought
of the little window came to me. I stopped :
bent : looked. She was standing as I had
left her by the table, but her face was
turned as towards the window. Large upward tearful eyes whose gaze was where ?
with me in that place if somewhere far
away ? . . . *Should I go back to her ?* . . .

I lifted up my head and went on slowly
to the door, with a foreboding in me. Of
what ? I opened the door : was out : had
half drawn it to, when the thought of
Wasn't it all a dream ? hastened my draw-

ing to, and the noise of the met jambs took
a deeper noise in the staircase. I was at
the first step : my left foot on the second :
my right on the third. I felt a pain there.
My ankle had been hurt : true.

I went down.

As I got into the cab opposite the door,
I looked up at our balcony half hoping to
see her there. No. Nor at the window.

Once more, as we drove away, I looked up
at balcony and window. No. I was a fool.

I thought much on our way to the Gare
du Nord.

When we arrived there I found that I
had abundance of time. I began to walk
up and down the hall, thinking profoundly.
At last this thought came : ' The next
evening I met the Professor at the Gare du
Nord as we had arranged, and (he, at the end
of our walk up and down in the hall ——
There we turned, there he began to speak
—-commending Rosy to my care as a last
sudden thought that . . .'

Sudden thoughts came quickly. I

paced up and down more quickly. A
porter with my portmanteau came to me
to remind me that it was time to be getting
my luggage weighed and myself on to the
platform. We went up the hall together.
I looked at the clock. He was right. I
gave one big step on, and suddenly stopped.
He passed me, and stopped too, but not as
I had done.

'Thanks:' I said. 'I shall not go to-
night.'

'Good, sir,' he said.

'If you will put that into a cab,' I said,
'I will be back in a moment.'

'Very well, sir,' he said.

I went off to the telegraph office, where
I wrote on a form: *Lady Gwatkin, 22,
Balmoral Street, London,* and *B. Leicester,
Paris,* and *I cannot come.* Then, when the
clerk had shown me that he understood it
aright, I returned to my porter and the
portmanteau in the cab. I thought much
on our way to the Avenue de Fontenoi.
When we arrived there I, who had not, did

not look up at either balcony or window, got out with my portmanteau and, having paid the man, went slowly in. As the impulse to look up had been denied, so was that to ask at the concierge's if she had gone out. But the concierge came forth to proffer carrying up the portmanteau : and I surrendered it to him. Up, then, I went slowly, deliberately, with mechanical limping foot. At the second story some one came out, a man, and descended upon me : when, through the mutual choosing of first one side and then the other, there was a moment's delaying till I went straight on, but not before I had, in the gas-light, caught a mechanical glimpse of a face that mechanically reminded me of some one. I cared not. Up I went again slowly, deliberately, with mechanical limping foot ; till I reached our third story, and the door, and had unlocked it, and gone in, and drawn it to quietly. The passage in the red light of the hanging oil lamp's little floating redder core flame. No : not to look in at the small window.—In here, into the study. Almost dark : no one here.

Now into the salon. Almost dark too : no one here. Don't call for her, or your voice will unnerve you as a concession to the ghostly.

In the morning-room. Almost dark : no one.

In the bedroom : no one.

Will you go into the bath-room ? Yes. No one.—Stand and think a little.

Now go back through all those almost dark and empty rooms, restraining that cry that is in the top of your beating heart. And, going back, *what an emptiness there is in the place !*

It is foolish to feel the presence of the ghostly or something seeably unseen here. The matches are on the mantlepiece behind the jar. Don't knock it over, you groper.— Light. No : darkness. These thin contraband matches are better than the stinking sulphurs, but still . . . Out again. *Damn !*

Now be careful this time. Light the candle.

It is lit.

What is the time ? A quarter to nine. Now—— A letter on the table.

She is gone !

My mouth is dry : I swallow. Read the letter. Here :—

' Mr. LEICESTER.

'I warned you of it. I see it all now. I told you I would go away when it came. The last thing I ask from you is for me never to see you again. You will find everything in the house. I have only taken the clothes I have on and £2 7s., which I had when I went with you. You are not to try to find me. If you do, you are a coward and no gentleman. I pray God will forgive me for my wickedness; He knows I did not do it for gain, but for pure love for you ; that is the only comfort I have within myself. I loved you, but what is love and how strong when through

suffering hate takes the place of that love.
I hate you and I always shall.

'R. H.'

I sat down and, with my elbows on my
knees and my head between my hands,
tried to think it out.

CHAPTER IV.

DESPITE every effort that was made to discover her, Rosy remained undiscovered. At the end of a week I made my arrangements in the matter and crossed over to London, where I felt sure I should ultimately have news of her. I had been informed by a chief of the Parisian police that either she had got off by the very train which I had intended to take, or else she was dead. I felt a strong conviction that neither had she got off by that train (how was it possible?), nor yet was she dead; but at times a horrible idea came over me that she might be being detained in some infamous den. This chief of police had confidently assured me that it was not so: I had, myself, wandered

about in filthy back streets enough in the
forlorn hope of finding her : had at last,
thinking of Marina, visited infamous dens
enough, places of hot air and bright light
and tawdrily rich ornament, filled with
fat and ghastly painted naked women who
had at first almost terrified me, thinking of
that awful breathless picture of Juvenal's
Agrippina, and then made me sorrowful
nigh to tears. And here in this London,
where my own poor mother had offered her
body for sale in the public way ; what a
thought was it to think, that perhaps I had
not persevered enough in that search ;
perhaps if I had stayed another week,
another *day*, I might have found her!
Thought of it and recollection of it mingled
perpetually. I could do no steady work.
As day followed day, and still no news
either from Parisian or London police, I
became so feverish at nights that I could
not sleep.

At last, one evening about a fortnight
after she had left me, sitting in my easy-

chair in the study window, trying to read a book, I began to think about the little canary (up there asleep in his cage), singing snatches of song, while the sun was on our feet, and, realizing once more that all this was not done in a dream, but that she was indeed gone from me, might at this moment be in misery, might die without my ever seeing her again—the tears came, and then, bowing my head down between my hands, I sobbed and wept. These were the first tears I had shed. They were a relief to me. I began to think of it as I had not yet thought of it, quietly and fully.

That night, for the first time since she had left me, I had a dreamless refreshing sleep. In the morning I went down the river to Greenwich again, and up onto the heath, thinking of Rayne, as I had so many times this last fortnight. The place seemed somewhat strange to me now: stranger than it had seemed before. I did not go to the school and the field where

Wallace and I had lain and played at 'chuck,' looking out at times over the dark, silver-twining Thames and duskily, far-reaching London.—I determined that I would find out about Rayne when I got back.

I went to Balmoral Street, and, seeing no assuring sign in No. 22 of life or death, rang, and inquired of a maid who opened the door, if Lady Gwatkin was any better? There was no surprise in her face. *Rayne was not dead.* My breath flowed out almost in a sigh.—Lady Gwatkin was a good deal better. She had gone with Sir James into the country.

It was enough. Further words I did not hear. I went away almost joyfully.

A few days later, I saw Strachan, and spoke about the Expedition, Starkie, Clarkson and Brooke, again. Worked with a will at my classics, and at my spiritual classics as well: struggled against despondent and not-to-be-dismissed thoughts about Rosy. Once was almost setting out for Paris, with a notion (illogical enough) that she was there, but a little thought showed me that my arrangement of things was best. She was in London I was sure. She would probably write to me in Paris (perhaps not knowing my London address). My man would telegraph at once : I would be with her at once. But a sudden idea that my man might, after all, be negligent, unsettled me.

It was the afternoon after this consideration of the matter in which the sudden idea of my man perhaps being negligent had occurred to me, that I spent in a long walk and debate.

When I returned home, looking as usual on the hall table for the longed-for telegram, I saw one. (My heart started.) I picked it up, and came quietly into the study and, at the window, opened it.

She was found.

I threw up my face and laughed. *Found ! found ! found !* Found at last.

A letter from her. (Address unnoticed yet.) This:

'*I cannot give you up. I am ill. Do come to me. I am sorry for it. It was wrong of me. Will you forgive me and come?*

'*R. H.*'

' Forgive you ? Come ?' I said, laughing. ' Oh, little Rosebud. I will forgive you for forgiving me ! I will come to you, and keep you, and——' Ending in tearful laughter.

To have found her again ! To know that I had not . . . Nay, I knew nothing yet ! And she was ill.

How long it took for that gold-incited hansom to get to the place ! How long the Anglicized Italian woman took to tell me where she was ! Upstairs I went at last : up, up, to the very top of the house, the dusty, dingy attic. She was there.

I knocked softly at the door and, on *her* voice saying that I was to come in, went in, and stood for a moment looking. I had but seen her pale worn face on the pillow before she had started up with a glad cry. And then I was holding her in my arms, and she me, silently.

In a little I felt that my eyes were full of tears; but she squeezed me in her old dear child's way, so quietly, pulling me in to her: and the smiles came to my lips, and I bent back my head so as to look at her face. But she would not let me: turning round her head and pressing it to my neck, in her old dear child's way. It seemed a dream that we had ever been away from one another. And then all at once she kissed me on the lips, such a long kiss: and hid her face again, and sighed contentedly. And so we remained in one another's arms some time—silently.

At last I began to think; but had no more than begun, when her breast heaved, all her body heaved, before the sound of the cough came as a relief to it. I feared that my holding her might increase the

effort, and made a little move to loosen
from her, but she would not. *Feared*
indeed : there was fear in me.

'Rosebud,' I said, when I was sitting by
her on the bed, stroking her hand, she
lying back on the pillow looking at me,
' you've got a very bad cold.'

'Yes,' she said ; 'I——' And went off
into another fit of coughing, the third she
had had since I came in. It was fear-
inspiring to listen to her.

'How did you get it ?' I asked.

'Got it !' she said with a smile. 'Caught
it !'

'Well——' I began : and stopped. I
was determining that she should be out of
London before that night.

And so she was.—We went down together to Micklehurst, a place I had heard
of as being sunny and with a deep blue
sky. The child seemed very contented,
quietly contented, dreamily contented, somewhat contented as I did not quite like her
to be. The patience with which she bore

her convulsive fits of coughing seemed to
me strange. Once I caught myself thinking
of a dying monkey I had seen in Paris
streets.

Arrived in the hotel, albeit I hesitated
a little, I determined that I would go and
bring a doctor to see her. And, having
made her comfortable in the window at a
room that looked over the blue winding
seay river, with its girdling darkened
mountains, over which the sun was setting
in mellow golden warmth, I went down
and inquired the name and address of some
doctor. I seemed to be drinking in the
clear, pure air as I walked along.

I found the doctor's house, and the
doctor : and brought him to see her. He
reported a bad cold, cautiously adding that
he would come again and see her on
Saturday. (This was Wednesday.) I accompanied him down to the hotel door.
I rather liked his face : he had a little gold
light in his eyes somewhere, perhaps something to do with the sun there. I asked

him one or two questions about her which
he answered simply. She had caught a
bad cold : that was clear. Perhaps it was
nothing more: perhaps again it was, perhaps
even it might develop into congestion.
She seemed in rather a low state of health;
but he would see her again in a few days,
on Saturday, and then he should be able to
tell me if there was anything. I said :

'Thank you; very well, be it so. My
name is Leicester. We shall probably be
staying here for some little time.'

And so we parted.

Rosy spent a bad night with the coughing.
She did not care to go out, although
the day was delightfully sunnily warm, but
stayed in an easy-chair by the open window
looking over the blue winding scay river
and the girdling mountains, all set in the
deep blue enamelled firmament. I left her
with a book for an hour in the morning
and went down onto the shore : and again,
late in the afternoon. Her cough grew
worse towards evening, and at last it struck

me to go out and get her some sweets to suck to try and stop it. I brought in a large packet of divers sorts, which pleased her: and we sat by the fire, which she had wished should be lit, and talked quietly and happily about ourselves of the past. It seemed a dream that we had ever been away from one another; but a sweet soft dream that had sweetened and softened all the time that we had been with one another.

This night was worse than the last, and the next day than that which preceded it: and so with the next night. Two or three times this night, after a long fit of convulsive coughing, she brought up some sticky, rusty-coloured stuff, with thin streaks of blood in it, that I examined in the candle-light, and having examined, felt a renewal of that indefinable fear that had entered me when all her body heaved before the sound of the cough came as a relief to it. As I lay back, thinking about this, she all at once said :

'I think I'm going to die.'

I was startled.

After a pause :

'What makes you think that?' I said.

After another pause :

'I wanted to die. I knew I was catching it all the while, and I didn't care : I didn't stop it. That was because I wanted to die. But when I found how . . . I think God is going to punish me for it.'

I turned over, and smiling, gave her a kiss on the cheek.

'Serious,' she said, moving her head a little and looking at me. 'Serious.'

'Quite serious,' said I, beginning to laugh. 'Quite serious, you ——' and chucked her under the chin. An unfortunate act ; for immediately succeeded a violent fit of coughing, and an unsuccessful attempt to get up some more of the sputa.

That inspection of the handkerchief ultimately decided me at breakfast to go and find the doctor again : which I did, but he could not come till later.

Rosy was informed that she would have to go to bed again, and perhaps have to stop there a little. I at once suspected congestion, whatever that precisely meant.

As the doctor and I went down together I catechized him. He said that she had pneumonia. I inquired the precise meaning of pneumonia.

'Inflammation of the substance of the lungs.'

'Was it dangerous?'

'Sometimes.'

'Fatal?'

'Sometimes.'

'How long did it last?'

'Three or four days, in good cases; more generally a fortnight or so.'

I asked him a few more questions, and then he took up the word, and told me what would, what might be required to, be done. Then we parted.

I came upstairs to Rosy again, with a

feeling as if there was going to be a species of campaign undertaken. The first thing to do was to find out if she minded leaving the hotel. She did not. Then I went out to observe the house that the doctor had recommended to me.

It was rather a cottage than a house. I liked it. It had a small garden, bright with flowers, in front of the dining-room, a long thin room with two door-windows opening on to a little lawn. I came back with a description of it, which, having pleased her, sent me off to take the place at once : and back to bring her to it.

By lunch-time we, I and the landlady and the servant, had the dining-room turned into a bed-room—light, airy, and comfortable.

The doctor came in the afternoon again. Further directions were given, and he left us, saying that he would leave the prescriptions at the chemist's as he went home. By tea-time everything was ready. Rosy had throughout remained quiescent, except that, as she was coming into the house, she had noticed some red daisies in the bed under the window, and plucked one, saying : 'A pretty thing !' and for a moment stood looking at it, while I stood looking at her.

I had every thing to hand—inhaler, medicines, milk, beef-tea : and the kettle, with a long brown-paper spout to it, so as to keep the atmosphere moist with the steam, on the fire, from whose immediate heat and light she was sheltered by the bed-curtain drawn out and tucked under the mattress. The idea of nursing her was, of course, pleasing to me. I felt no fear now. The sense of her lying there as she was, seemed to admit of no feeling but calm tenderness.

The cough was very troublesome : more violent, more as it were ineffectual. She was very thirsty, and complained of the warm milk and beef-tea. Orders had been left that it was to be warm, and so of course she would have to drink it warm. I had to coax her to it like a child. The same with the inhalation. At first she,

half sleepy, would not draw, but kept
moaning, and turning her mouth away
from the pipe, till I bantered her into
taking twenty pulls to show she was not
afraid of it, and then turned the twenty
into thirty, and the thirty into fifty, and so
on up to a hundred, and far over (I de-
ceiving her by dropping back ten several
times) : and so the requisite ten minutes
inhaling were achieved. She could get no
sleep. She kept up this low moaning all the
while, occasionally sitting up with her chin
on her knees, and the lower part of her
hands in her eyes. Once she suddenly
looked up at me and said :

' Don't you believe I got this as a punishment for wanting to die ?'

' No ; I don't. I think you got it as the
very natural result of catching a severe cold.'

' But I did it —I did it on purpose.'

' The cold wouldn't know anything about
that. There now ! Now you've asked
what you wanted to ask, and you mustn't
talk any more.'

She had a violent fit of coughing. When it was done she said :

'I do wish you'd talk to me. I cannot get to sleep. I like to hear you talking.'

'Very well,' I said. 'I'll tell you a story. Will that do ?'

'Yes,' she said. 'But lie down there. I don't like you sitting up.'

I lay down on the extreme edge of the bed, with my head on the bolster, and began my story. It was the story of Undine. Often I had to stop on account of her coughing. Once the story was so broken into by a fit of coughing, that I hoped she would forget or not care to hear any more ; would try to go to sleep. Not so. She began to talk about what had happened to her in London, and would not brook interruption. At last, I let her say what she had to say. She told me of her life at Wiltshire Crescent.

'I was glad when you came,' she said slowly, with pauses. 'I had a most horrid

dream of you. I dreamed you were dead,
and that I saw your coffin carried by
men to the cemetery. I thought I was
in such grief about parting with you in
anger, that I would have given half my life
to have parted with you friendly . . . I
know I have been very wicked in doing
what I have, but I do believe God will
forgive me. I did love you. I was also
in trouble as to whether you were safe in
heaven, and I thought I wept so bitterly,
and my grief was so great that, while I was
following to see where you were buried, I
was obliged to kneel down to pray God to
take you to heaven, and to forgive all, at
the same time promising I would be good
all the rest of my life, in hope to see you
there : when I awoke and found it all a
dream. I was very pleased, but it upset
me for days, and at last I made up my
mind to write to you, as I could not rest.
Well, *there !* it's all over now : and very
likely it' *I* am going to die instead of
you.'

Here she had another fit of coughing, and I got up to give her some milk. After that I felt she had forgotten the story, but she requested its continuance, and so I continued it, with the necessary breaks, till four in the morning, when she fell asleep. Not even the orders of the doctor, that is to say my duty, prevailed over my disinclination to awakening her at five for her medicine. She herself awoke a little later: the medicine was given : and at her request the story continued ; but only for a little, for we could not get on with it ' one little bit,' as she said, owing to the growing frequency of her fits of coughing. She was quite exhausted by the time the sun came into the room over the top of the hedge : about seven o'clock. I was tired, but not sleepy : and less tired when I had washed myself. Then she got a little sleep.

The doctor came about eleven. He sanctioned her drinking her milk and beef tea cold if she really did not like to drink it warm : and Rosy's silence said that she

really did not like.   I went with him to the
door and into the garden, where I asked him
if he could not give her some opiate.   He
shook his head.   I said that she was being
torn to pieces by the cough, and that I
could not help thinking that it was dangerous to let her get as exhausted as she had
been a few hours ago, and was yet.   He
said :

'I dare not give her anything.'

The words and their tone settled the
matter.   I asked again if it was possible to
give her any stimulants now ?   He said :

'No ; best not.   Go on just the same as
yesterday with the inhaler and the poultices,
and the milk and beef-tea.   That is all.'

I said that as fast as I gave it her, she
brought it all up again : purposelessly.
Then, after a proposal about a nurse,
which I refused, he left me.   I thought no
more of him.

At about five she would have me lie
down on the edge of the bed and try to get
some sleep : and, with the promise from

her that she would awaken me in an hour, when it would be time for her to inhale again, I closed my eyes. She deceived me. It was seven when I awoke: was awakened by what was, maybe, an unusually violent fit of coughing. I scolded her, dear little Rosebud, so thin-faced now, as I got the inhaler ready: she, between her coughings, smiling at me.

After tea—I sitting by the bedside, holding her hand and thinking—she all at once, quite opened her eyes and looked at me:

'Where do people go to when they die?' she said.

I looked at her dear child's eyes, but did not answer her.

'Do tell me,' she said, in a child's aggrieved tone, rumpling her brow. 'Don't tease me! Tell me true.'

After a pause, in which memory dwelt lovingly on look and tone, and that sweet correlating gesture of the hidden face, I answered her:

'I believe that they go into the earth from which they came.'

'Yes,' she said, ' but that's not their spirits. What do their spirits do?'

'Their spirits, too, go into the earth.'

She shook her head:

'No,' she said; ' their spirits go up'— (looking up)—'up into heaven.'

I lifted her hand, and bent my head, and kissed her hand softly.

'But don't *you* think so too?' she said.

'No,' I said, still bent over her hand. 'But' (looking up at her and smiling), 'what does it matter *what* I think, dear?'

She began to cough, and went on for a little. Then:

'Don't you think,' she said, 'that good people go to heaven when they die?'

'Now don't you talk any more in this way!" I said, getting up and sitting on the bed by her, 'or I shall—well, I shall have to stop you someway.' And I put my arm round her shoulders.

'Ah,' she said, drawing her head back so as to look at me, ' but don't you ?'

' Don't I what ?'

Her brow rumpled.

' Don't tease me !' she said. ' You *must* tell me.'

' Very well,' I said, ' I will tell you, then. I don't think anyone goes to heaven, however good they are, for I don't believe there's any heaven to go to.'

' But what becomes of them, then ?'

' They go into the earth from whence they came.'

' That's horrid !' she said. ' I don't——' and began to cough again.

I put my arm round her shoulders, and leant my cheek to hers that was wet, while the lump gathered in my throat, and the tears in my eyes also.

' What is it, dear ?' I said. ' Why are you crying ?'

In a little :

' I was thinking,' she said, ' that God wouldn't let us see one another then, perhaps, because we had been so sinful, and because you—because you talked in that way. If you didn't talk in that way, perhaps He would, you know; because I *did* love you so!' (She had turned and thrown her arms round my neck.) 'Oh, I couldn't do without you! I did try, I did try. But you were so . . .' Her trembling lips did not finish it.

At last:

'Oh, Rosy,' I said, with a low, choking voice, 'what have I done to you? . . . Oh, my little Rosebud!'

'Hush!' she said, 'hush, dear; don't say that. I don't think God'll be so hard upon us; I don't think He will. And it wasn't *your* fault, this. It was all my fault; I did it. I knew I did. But I don't mind now. Kiss me, dear; kiss me. It wasn't your fault.'

I kissed her, and straightway the cough caught and shook her poor body through and through; but she would not have me take my arms from round her. And as I felt all this, the thought in me turned to utter fierceness.

We talked no more of these things, except that Rosy told me that last night she had dreamt of being smothered by wreaths of smoke, and could not wake me. We talked of the dear hours in the past, and of the dearer that were to be in the future—by snatches; for her cough was almost ceaseless, and, it seemed to me, more violent than last night. She had, apparently, forgotten about the story, which was to have been continued to-night; and I did not care to remind her of it while we were talking as we were of the dear hours in the past, and of the dearer that were to be in the future.

But, as the night wore on, she became worse. I had great trouble to get her to take the inhalation. She kept up the low moaning all the time, as she had done on the first night; occasionally, too, sitting up with her chin on her knees, and the lower part of her hands in her eyes. I did not

leave the bed-side for a moment. Now and
then she fell asleep, but the low moaning
did not cease, except when she muttered
incoherently.

The slow hours passed. I must have
dozed. I awoke with a start. She was
struggling violently. I saw that, and her
swollen, livid face, and eyes strangely
prominent with strange, clear brightness.
Then I knew that she wanted me, and, in a
moment, was across the bed, with one arm
round her body and the other loosening her
nightdress at the throat ; but she had caught
it, as it were, by chance, and rent it down
wide open, just as the button was coming
undone. I held her steadily up, despite her
violent, downward struggles. She knew I
was holding her. She could not get breath ;
she was suffocating. Her chest seemed
rigid. I looked at her livid face again, with
eyes of prominent, strange, clear brightness,
her stretched nostrils.

Then, before I scarcely knew what had
happened, except a tightened effort of her

body in my arms, she had ceased struggling. I looked at her face : looked long ; at last, wildly. I shook her gently ; lowered my arm to shake her again, when her head fell back with the upward, staring eyes. I put up a hand over, and closed and held them down ; and thought, *She is dead, dead.* What did that mean ? No. . . . No. . . .

I gathered her close in my arms, kissing her warm, pure throat and talking to myself ; and, at last, let both of us lie back in the soft pillows, I with my cheek on her warm, pure breast. Ah! better to sleep now without more words ; better to sleep. Think no more of that phantasy. I was given to such. Even as a boy, I could not quite tell sometimes whether I was in a dream or awake ; so now, I could not quite tell sometimes whether I had seen things in dreams or in the vital air : so now. But that was enough of speaking. Better to sleep now without more words ; better to sleep.

' *A bundle of myrrh is my well-beloved unto me ; he shall lie all night betwixt my breasts. I charge you, O ye daughters of Jerusalem, by the roes and by the hinds of the field that ye stir not up nor awake my love till he please.*'

THE END.

BILLING AND SONS, PRINTERS, GUILDFORD.